Letters of Blood

THE LIBRARY OF BANGLADESH

RIZIA RAHMAN

Letters of Blood
A Novel

TRANSLATED BY ARUNAVA SINHA

CALCUTTA LONDON NEW YORK

Seagull Books, 2018

Original © Rizia Rahman, 2016

Translation © Arunava Sinha, 2016

ISBN   978 0 8574 2 499 0

THE LIBRARY OF BANGLADESH series was conceived by
the Dhaka Translation Center at the University of Liberal Arts Bangladesh.
Find out more at http://dtc.ulab.edu.bd/

Printed in arrangement with Bengal Lights Books

This edition is not for sale in Bangladesh

British Library Cataloguing-in-Publication Data
A catalogue record for this book is available from the British Library

Typeset and designed by Sunandini Banerjee, Seagull Books, using artwork
by Narottama Dobey and W. Basher from the Bengal Lights editions

Printed and bound by Maple Press, York, Pennsylvania, USA

LIBRARY OF BANGLADESH
An Introduction

The independence of Bangladesh, while into its fifth decade now, is still viewed by many outsiders as an accident of history. All historical outcomes are in part an accident, but any event of the magnitude of Bangladesh's liberation can only happen as a consequence of deep and long-term agency. What underlies that agency in this case most decisively is a unique cultural identity.

Like the soft deposits flowing down from the Himalayas that created the land mass known as Bangladesh today, its culture too has resulted from centuries of diverse overlay. Generations here have always gravitated towards the mystical branch of the reigning faith, be it Buddhism, Hinduism or Islam. The net effect is a culture that has always valued tolerance and detachment over harsh rituals or acquisitive fierceness.

There is no way better than Bangladesh's literature to know what makes this unique and vital culture as full as it is of glory and, of course, foibles. How did a rain-washed delta full of penniless peasants turn into a leader among developing nations? How did the soft, mystical, Baul-singing population turn into one of the fiercest guerilla armies of the last century? How did love of the Bangla language trigger the very march to freedom? How do the citizens of the world's most densely populated city, barring only a few tax or gambling enclaves, make sense of daily life, and find any beauty, amid all the breathless din of commerce and endless jostle of traffic?

The first three books in this series provide a remarkable window into the realities and mindscape of this amazing, confounding, rich world through translations of three of the living legends of Bangladeshi writing: Syed Shamsul Haq, Hasan Azizul Huq and Syed Manzoorul Islam. The presentation of their work has been made possible by the Dhaka Translation Center, hosted by the University of Liberal Arts Bangladesh. It also owes a great deal to the tireless efforts of its Director, Kaiser Haq. The series owes most, however, to award-winning translator Arunava Sinha, who both helped conceive of this idea, and helms it as series editor. Eminent translators brought together by him have ensured a rare and truly world-class rendition of these hidden gems of world literature. The impressive international-standard production owes everything to DTC's sister concern, Bengal Lights, led by editor Khademul Islam and managing editor, QP Alam.

Bangladesh, for all its success, is still to the world the sum of half-told stories told by others. It's high time to offer a fuller account of ourselves to the world. DTC plans to bring out at least three titles each year, and add both new names and new titles by selected authors to this defining series on Bangladeshi writing. We also believe that the process of consciously engaging new and wider audiences will lead to new refinements to a body of work that is already one of the great overlooked treasures of global writing.

KAZI ANIS AHMED
Publisher, Bengal Lights Books
Founder, Dhaka Translation Center

AUTHOR'S NOTE

When I was in school, there was a girl in my class named Marjina. She was a wayward girl, a bit older than the rest of us. One day during the lunch break, she asked me, "What do you know about whores?" When I asked, surprised, "What's a whore?" she made fun of me. "Oh, poor little baby! You read all those storybooks and know about so many things, but you have no clue what a whore is! They go in packs to cinema halls to look for customers." I was annoyed. "What rubbish! I am not interested in listening to this filth."

Some days later, I went to the cinema with my mother. There was a woman sitting just one row ahead of us who looked a little different. She was thin and dark-skinned and very dressed up. The way she was sitting also seemed strange. After a while, she started making odd gestures towards the male members of the audience. She was continuously unbuttoning her blouse and then buttoning it back up again. She also kept pulling her sari up over her knees and then letting it down. I asked my mother why she was behaving that way. She scolded me, "Don't look in that direction again!" Disobeying her strict instructions, I kept looking at her out of the corner of my eyes. At one point, she took off both her sari and her blouse. Wearing just her bra and petticoat, she climbed up on to the seat. I cried out, "Look, Amma, look! She's taken her clothes off!" My mother didn't say anything but made me switch seats with her. I could no longer see the bizarre actions of that strange woman from my new position. When we got home, my mother confided to my cousin (who happened to be her age) "It's impossible for civilised folk to go to the cinema these days. Now it's become a gathering place for all sorts of nasty people, like whores. Tsk! Tsk! They were doing such dirty things!" That was the first time the word "whore" stuck in my head. I didn't really understand why whores did nasty things or why my mother didn't want them at the cinema. But I have no reason to deny that I had experienced a kind of pang upon seeing the wretched, scrawny face of that woman. I couldn't bring myself to hate her the way my mother did. Even now, I feel a twinge thinking back to the miserable, penniless prostitute and her desperate attempts to entice customers.

Anyway, after that day I assumed that sad, starving women in tattered clothing were called "whores." Some days later, I was walking to a relative's house with my mother. A slender woman walked past us. Not wanting to miss an opportunity to prove my sagaciousness, I said, "Look Amma! There goes a whore!" Not only was my comment greeted with a slap from my mother, I also had to endure the woman's rebuke. My mother exclaimed angrily, "You're just a little child, where did you pick up such a dirty word?" From my mother's reprimand, I figured out that "whore" was a swear word, a particularly nasty one. Years later, during one of those forbidden discussions of adolescence, Marjina reminded me what "whore" meant. At that time, I recollected, somewhat hazily, the pitiful face of that woman from the cinema.

Rokter Okkhor—a novel about the overlooked, miserable and tormented lives of women of an illicit part of society—brought me great fame in my writing career. I never imagined that I would write a book about something like this. The precocious, errant Marjina didn't know that my mother had taught me to hate prostitutes. Perhaps I myself did not realise I had unconsciously etched the forlorn face of that prostitute in my mind from that early age. Perhaps that face has acted as subconscious inspiration.

I wrote *Rokter Okkhor* almost thirty years ago, after three of my novels had been well received by readers. At that time, the weekly magazine *Bichitra* was very popular in Dhaka. The magazine once published a cover story titled "The Prostitutes of Dhaka" which presented, in great detail, the day-to-day lives of prostitutes in brothels. I was heartbroken after reading the piece; I couldn't sleep that night and headed to the *Bichitra* office the very next morning. Back then, the editor of the magazine was Shahadat Chowdhury. I asked him, "Tell me, is this truly what the life of a prostitute is like? Reading your article really pained me. Such contempt for human life!" At one point in our conversation, Shahadat said, "Apa, since you're so moved by this subject, why don't you write a novel on it?" I said, in that case I would have to get to know them even better. But, at that time, thirty years ago, it was not very easy to go into a brothel for information. Even expressing curiosity about whores was dangerous. Shahadat suggested I talk to some of the young reporters who had worked on the story. One of them was Shahriar Kabir, who told me that I should visit a brothel and observe the situation first-hand. I decided I would go.

I asked another journalist I knew, who worked for the *Robbar* magazine of *Ittefaq*, to take me. He said he couldn't do it, that he couldn't take responsibility for ensuring my safety. He said, "You have no idea how unsafe those places are. You're young and good-looking. Anything could happen! Then the newspaper headlines would be, 'Novelist Missing in Brothel.' You won't be able to go there. It's better if you get help from reporters instead." So he started bringing me weekly reports.

To be honest, I never met or spoke directly with any of the prostitutes. Back then, they were not allowed in regular society, just as we were not allowed inside brothels. It was particularly impossible for women to enter brothels—the environment was filthy and there was no security. I was shown enlarged photos of brothels taken by the *Ittefaq* journalists—of the living areas, kitchens etc. I looked at a number of photos and slowly developed the setting for my novel in my mind. Since I was gathering information from others while I was writing the novel, the news spread. Many well-known male writers of that time made fun of me, questioning what a woman could write on such a subject. A male acquaintance asked me, "You're writing about a sensitive issue, what if it comes back to hurt you? We're living under a military government. The authorities will no doubt be displeased."

All those discouraging comments frightened me greatly. I was under so much mental pressure that I stopped writing. I had been writing with such passion that I went into a sort of depression. At this point, my husband said to me, "Don't pay attention to these people. Just keep writing. We'll see what happens afterwards." He encouraged me and helped me get back my nerve. I resumed writing. The story was published in *Bichitra*. I never imagined the book would become so popular. It created such a stir! Everyone had the same question—how did I write such a novel. After I had finished the book, I asked one of the *Ittefaq* reporters who used to bring me information to take a copy to the brothel and give it to any literate girl he could find there for her to read. I wanted them to realise that they were human beings, just like everyone else. The reporter took the book but then I didn't hear back from him. So I contacted him one day and asked what had happened, why hadn't he given me any feedback. He replied, "Apa, I didn't have guts to tell you what they said." I insisted he still tell me. He said, "They asked which brothel the writer of the book was from." I became very angry. I had written the book in order to raise awareness about their rights, and they insult me like this in return! Then the reporter continued, "Apa, don't be upset. You don't realising what a huge compliment this is for you. Your writing is so flawless and lifelike that they automatically assumed such an account could not be written without having real experience."

I received a lot of praise for the book, but also had to endure an equal amount of abuse. I would receive offensive calls in the middle of night from all over the place. People would curse at me for writing about prostitutes. Even people I knew exclaimed, "Tsk! Tsk! How could a woman from a respectable family write such a story?" I became unwell again. Amidst all the appreciation and humiliation, two common questions arose: one, how did I write the story and two, why did I drag a character like Yasmin— an educated, well-to-do woman from a freedom fighter's family— into the middle of all of this ugliness? I even got calls from Kolkata. The answer to the first question is, this book is my protest, my voice against this dark side of society. I wanted to show everyone how intolerable the lives of these women are. It was intentional. After the book became popular, I realised that it had struck readers that prostitutes were people too. They must have thought at least once that, yes, prostitutes are also human beings. And the character of Yasmin was not completely imaginary. At that time, I had witnessed the state of Birangonas (women who were tortured physically and sexually by the Pakistani army and its collaborators during Bangladesh's liberation war) to be very similar. I told everyone, "Look, it's because she's a decent girl from a middle-class family, because she's like you, that it's bothering you so much. And those girls from poor families—Bokul, Kusum, Parul, who were lured with promises of jobs, or kidnapped, and then sold to brothels by brokers—doesn't your heart cry for them?" Many of them were sold off by their fathers or brothers because of poverty. They were born free. But they became commodities because the state couldn't ensure their basic human rights or feed them. I agree with what Rousseau said almost 300 years ago, that man is born free, and everywhere he is in chains. Once, a politician asked me why I was so concerned about those women. Prostitution was an established profession that had existed for thousands of years. I asked, "What do you mean, established profession?" Did these women choose this profession? Or did society force them, toss them into the gutter? And we pretend we know nothing. On top of everything, the money they earn—which isn't enough for them to even get by—adds to the national income and is used by the state for the development of our country. They even contribute to the cars that the ministers drive around in.

But the good thing is that now there are many NGOs across the world which work with this section of society. People's perspectives have also changed somewhat. Recognition is being given to their rights and entitlements. I had written the book many years ago, reflecting the situation back then. What is disappointing is that their actual condition has not really changed at all. In fact, their miserable state is just being re-wrapped. Our capitalist society has always used women as commodities. Now, because of pressure from various sources, prostitution is being legalised under a new label, "sex worker." Awareness campaigns are being carried out and other steps taken in order to prevent prostitutes from contracting AIDS or spreading it among their clients. It is similar to giving someone paracetamol to contain their fever as a temporary measure while ignoring the actual cause. To keep pace with the West, we are also calling such women sex workers. People have accepted it as a profession. I say, ask one of the girls whether they would rather work in a brothel or in a garments factory. She will never want to be a sex worker. So how can we pass it off as a profession? Even now, women are forced into this hell. The purpose for which I had written the novel has not been fulfilled. I am told that it is impossible to stop prostitution completely. I ask, "Why?" What if the authorities decide to punish not only those who take part in human trafficking or brokering, but also those who go to brothels as customers? When there is no demand for something, there will be no supply as well. Then the businessmen will not be able make profits or force these girls into this industry. Alas, no one has taken the initiative.

I thank Dhaka Translation Center and Bengal Lights Books for translating this book and taking my voice to an international level. I dedicate this novel to the rights of women and pose this question to the world: is it not a violation of human rights to force women into this so-called profession?

Dhaka, 2016

Letters of Blood

ONE

The morning lies here in an inert stupor like a drug addict. A faint beam of sunlight rolls as shamelessly as a non-paying customer around a wall with the plaster flaking off. Next to a drain overflowing with refuse, a gathering of crows is engaged in civil war over packets made with dry leaves and oil-soaked paper scraps. A mangy dog is curled up in sleep nearby. There are no other sounds.

Kusum has woken up quite early. She's the first to leave her bed in this area. Bokul, Jahanara, Sakina, Marjina and the other women are usually asleep at this hour, sprawled awkwardly. Mannan's shop deep in the lane won't be open yet. Only the young boy manning the dive across the road selling *dalpuri* and *golgolla* will be lighting the stove.

The toilet that everyone uses will soon see a queue like at the ration store. Then pots, pitchers and buckets for water will begin to pile up next to the draw-well on the ground slippery with moss. A battle will begin. Quarrels, screams and obscenities will ring in everyone's ears. Meanwhile, old Golapjaan's constant coughing can be heard. The hag starts coughing before sunrise. She dumps herself just about anywhere these days. Today, she's a lump of flesh outside the door of Rupa, Amina and Moti's house, lying on the bricks where the cement has worn off. Everyone knows Golapjaan used to ply her trade here once upon a time. Later she became a madam. Now she has nothing to call her own besides her ribs and crippled body. When a hint of a dim, murky light appears between the rows of dilapidated buildings a little later in the day, Golapjaan wakes up and crawls about outside the doors. Staring greedily at the girls with their glasses of tea and *dalpuris*, she holds her hand out. "Give me some?"

Sakina snarls, slamming her glass down on the floor, "Why don't you die, you witch? You think we have enough to eat? Five customers in three days."

Sakina and her sister are in the trade. Their mother, aunt and grandmother used to be in the trade too.

Throwing a glance at Jahanara's closed door, Sakina barks, "Why, you toothless whore, why don't you go to Jahanara? Changes her dress a hundred times a day. Buys dozens of pitchers of water. Has a servant. Arrogant bitch."

The other doors begin to open, one by one. The girls emerge from all directions. Kusum draws a bucket of water from the well for a wash. Stale green putrid water.

Mashi says, "You don't think there's any water in that well anymore, do you? It's rotting human blood in there."

Mashi has seen corpses of murdered people thrown into the well.

Kusum doesn't care. She has not yet attained the status of getting Thika Mashi—the part-time maid—to buy her water from the tap on the main street. Her fourteen-year-old under-nourished body hasn't amassed enough capital.

Splashing half a can of water on her face, Kusum enters her room. The other two have woken up. Sitting up, Shanti yawns. Wrapping a half-dirty sari around her bare body, she gives Zarina a shove. "Wake up, Zari, you bitch. How long will you sleep?"

Shaking Shanti's hand off, Zarina hugs the oil-stained pillow to herself and turns on her side leisurely.

Shanti makes a face. "Such airs! Like you laid dozens of men all night."

Taking a cigarette out from under her pillow, she lights it. Turning to Kusum, she says, "*Oi* Kusmi, go see if Thika Mashi has come. If she has, tell her to get me two *dalpuris*."

Shanti throws a couple of notes at her. Both Shanti and Zarina operate independently in this room. They pay the rent themselves. Kusum's income belongs to Kalu. She is still under his control. Among them, Shanti is the one who earns the most. She has raised her rate. Her fortune is on the rise.

Kusum goes out with the money. She didn't get a customer yesterday. So, no food either at night. Who knows what today will bring.

Thika Mashi has arrived. She's busy ferrying water to different rooms from the tap on the main road. Many of the girls pay Babu for their *tehari* and *bakarkhani*, their favourite dishes of rice and beef and leaven bread. Babu has more or less become a permanent resident hereabouts. He used to be everyone's customer. He has rented a room now. He has a woman to himself. Babu is a decent man. He does chores whenever needed, brings them *tehari* and *bakarkhani* and naan. Of course, only a handful of girls order all this. Jahanara, Bokul and Manu eat meat twice a day, every day. They bathe twice too. They have other habits of the wealthy as well.

Kusum stops in front of Bokul's door. Thika Mashi plonks down a pot of water and calls out, "Where are you, *buji*? Give me my money. I have no time to wait."

Kusum can see a part of Bokul's room, for the door is ajar. This room belongs to her alone. She pays a rent of thirty taka a day and occupies it on her own. Bokul is one of the rising stars here. She has laid out a mattress on her cot. On her wall is a large square mirror with a floral design on the frame. There's even a photograph of Bokul's on the trunk painted with roses. All the girls hereabouts are keen on getting themselves photographed. Many of them go to the studio on the main road in their burqas and have themselves shot in various poses. Kusum has never been photographed. Let alone the studio, she is not even allowed to leave the lane.

Bokul appears at the door in a short red petticoat and a sleeveless blouse, her eyes heavy with sleep. Raising her arm and resting it on the doorframe, she says in irritation, "Why are you shouting loud enough to wake the dead, you bitch? Can't you see I have someone in here?"

Kusum peeps in to discover Bokul's regular customer sleeping in her bed.

Extracting a bidi from her waist, Thika Mashi lights it. Summoning a pleasant friendliness to her face, she bites her tongue in remorse, "Really? Give me my money, *bua*, I have to deliver water to others too."

Bokul flings some coins at her from inside the room. "Here. Fuck off now. Bokul never owes anyone any money."

Now Kusum gives the notes in her hand to Mashi. "O Mashi, Shanti Buji says to bring her two *dalpuris* and a cup of tea."

Picking up the coins Bokul threw at her, Mashi grumbles, "How many things am I supposed to do at the same time?"

Still, she takes the money from Kusum. Like Bokul, she has begun to be attentive to Shanti too these days. You never knew, what if she surpasses Bokul?

After Mashi leaves with the money, Kusum squats by the drain. The stench of rotting garbage rises from it. Kusum is dizzy. She starved yesterday too. Her stomach is churning. She sets her disinterested eyes on a slice of sky appearing like a straight line above the dilapidated buildings. The striped T-shirt she's wearing over her dirty pyjamas hasn't been washed in a fortnight. She's going to ask Shanti for some soap today. Worst comes to worst, she will pour a mug or two of the putrid water from the well over herself for a bath. Kusum looks enviously at Bokul's room. She could have had a body like Bokul's, couldn't she? How long before her thighs and breasts and buttocks acquire those proportions?

Zarina has told her, "All you need to do is eat properly to get some flesh on your body. You'll have customers fighting over you.

You can use hair oil like Shanti then, wear saris like Bokul, visit rich people's houses in the city in a car like Jahanara. Mashi will pay attention to you. Babu will bow and scrape before you. Kalu Sardar will request you to accept a cigarette. Make yourself a body, get some rice into your belly."

Leave alone eating properly, you can count on your fingers the number of times Kusum even gets a meal. She doesn't have independent earnings like Shanti or Zarina. It's been more than two years now that she has been working for a pimp. She has a right to a meal of daal and rice only if she gets customers. The client pays. She hands the money over to Boro Mashi, who gives it to Kalu.

Even yesterday, the demon delivered a couple of heavy kicks on her stomach. Pain still clots her abdomen. Kusum had stolen a taka from a customer a few days ago, hiding it in the tin of salt. She doesn't even get to see her daily earnings. And when she has no money to hand over, she gets no food. For two days, Kusum had had no customers, no earnings, no meals. Getting Thika Mashi to buy her some *muri*, she was sneaking into her room when Kalu had stormed in from nowhere. Snatching the packet with his paw, he had said, "You bitch! Where did you get the money, *maagi*?"

Kusum had paled with fear, fumbling for words as she stared at the dry scar on Kalu's forehead. She had said "Shanti Buji gave me."

Tossing the packet of *muri* into the drain, Kalu had grabbed a handful of Kusum's hair, twisting her body and flinging her to the ground. "You're lying, *haramjaadi*. How much money did you take from the customer? You gave the regular payment to Mashi. Where did you get this?"

Golapjaan the hag had crawled up to the drain to collect the grains of *muri*. Mad Karimon and Sakina's five-year-old daughter were also scrambling for them. Throwing a glance at the scene, Kusum had bit her lip. She had prepared herself, looking fearfully at Kalu's pockmarked face, bulging lips and scar on the forehead. What would Kalu do now? Would he hit her? She was often beaten up. Mashi says Kalu can kill a man without wiping the smile off his face. He had slapped her resoundingly, making her head reel. Thrown against the wall, Kusum had lifted her head. "I took it from the customer's pocket. Why shouldn't I? You think I don't want food too? You think I don't get hungry?"

By then, Kalu's slaps and kicks had drained Kusum's tiny body.

Everyone was busy with their lives. Laughing, eating, gossiping. No one had spared a glance for Kusum.

This is the system in this brothel. Kalu can kill the girls he's bought if he wants to. No one has the right to say anything.

A thin beam of sunlight throws a sickly glow on the crumbling wall. Shanti ambles up to the draw-well. Mashi has brought her two pitchers of water. Shanti is going to have a long leisurely bath now. Kusum throws a sidelong glance at Shanti's red velvet petticoat, washed sari, and fresh *gamchha*. Undoing her plaits, Shanti is singing, her bright soap-case resting on a brick. She loosens her sari. With a complexion on the fair side, Shanti has a round scar mark on her breast. Everyone knows its history. A wealthy customer had once pressed a burning cigarette on her skin. Not in anger, but in wild lust. Shanti is soaping her legs, her sari raised above her knees. Kusum looks away. People are passing in the lane. Some of the women have customers even at this hour. Kusum looks at the end of the lane hungrily. What if she got a well-paying customer right now?

Soaping her face, Shanti shouts, "Kusum, come here. Soap my back."

Kusum makes a face. "Here I am dying of hunger and you want me to soap your back."

Shanti giggles needlessly. "Oh my, so angry. Come on now, I have a *dalpuri* for you."

Lured by this assurance, Kusum goes up to her. Shanti is about twenty, with the body of a dancer in the movies. Rubbing soap into the smooth skin of her back, Kusum feels a surge of rage. She cannot stand this elaborate bathing ritual. Shanti takes a long time over her bath, pouring two pitchers of water slowly and luxuriously over herself. Like the calendars in Mannan's shop, Shanti's bathing is also lustrous. She twists and turns her body to give people a view from all angles. As though she's saying, "How many girls here have a body like mine? And how many can afford to bathe every day in water they buy for themselves?"

When her back is done, Shanti moves her wet petticoat aside to expose her thighs. "I'll soap, you pour."

Meanwhile, Babu and Mashi are having a furious argument.

Leaning with her back against the door, Bokul throws a sharp look at Shanti and shouts, "Get up now, *maagi*. How much more of your body do you want to flaunt?"

Instead of answering, Shanti giggles. Then, looking at Bokul's door, she says, "What are you afraid of? Your man won't look at me. You know all the tricks."

Averting her face, Kusum smiles too at this. She also knows what Shanti means. Bokul won't have a bath now. Once it's past twelve, she will take two buckets of water up the crumbling staircase to the roof. The dwelling houses across the road, the shops lining the street, the people passing by—all of them are visible from the open roof with no walls. Bokul has her bath in various attractive poses up there. It is this well-advertised bathing that has changed her fortunes. Now she smokes expensive cigarettes. Goes to the films every week. Picks and chooses her customers. But she hasn't yet given up her practice of bathing on the roof.

Finishing her bath, Shanti draws her *gamchha* to herself. She is still staring with narrowed eyes at Bokul's door. Bokul's man will emerge any moment. He is employed. Kusum follows Shanti's eyes. Bokul's door has opened. Her man comes out behind her. At once, Shanti moves her *gamchha* away from her breasts, raises her wet petticoat above her knees and begins to sing loudly:

> *Come my lover*
> *Stay my lover*
> *Why must you sigh*
> *Is my lover*
> *Angry now*
> *Is the rate too high*

Bokul's man pauses and then turns to stare openly at Shanti, who immediately signals to him seductively. The whole thing takes place in an instant. Elbowing her flirtatious customer aside, Bokul launches herself at Shanti. Kusum moves away apprehensively. Bokul flings Shanti's fancy soap-case and dry clothes into the drain and begins to rain kicks and punches on her while showering her with abuse. Shanti is not prepared for this onslaught. But she recovers in a flash and counter-attacks Bokul. Shanti is no pushover. A crowd gathers around their brawl. By then, both of Shanti's pitchers have broken. Blood is trickling from the corner of Bokul's lips. Her forehead is swollen. Mashi comes downstairs from her room. "Oh no! What are these two up to now? Let go. Look at you."

Neither of them is willing to let go. Mashi forces them apart. Shanti leaves for her room, mouthing obscenities, after gathering her soap-case and mud-splattered sari from the drain. Bokul stands outside her door, seething. No one has noticed when her man slipped away amidst the commotion. Going into her empty room, Bokul slams the door, threatening Shanti loudly through the locked door.

Kusum returns to her room slowly. Shanti is scraping the mud off her body with her *gamchha*, muttering angrily under her breath. Spotting Kusum, she says, "Go tell Babu to buy me pitchers from the market. And my name isn't Shanti if I don't smash that bitch's pride."

Her hunger begins to churn in Kusum's belly again. Greedily she notices a *dalpuri* on a plate in a corner of the room. Tugging at a dry sari on the clothesline, Shanti snarls at her, "What are you standing there for? Go fetch Babu."

Kusum whimpers, "My *dalpuri*?"

Shanti turns, looking furious. Throwing the *dalpuri* at Kusum, she says, "Here, shove it down your throat."

Kusum grabs it, rolls it up and stuffs it in her mouth. Zarina, who had gone out, comes into the room, laughing. "*Ki lo*, Shanti? I hear you gave good to that proud bitch?"

Shanti doesn't laugh. Taking the packet of cigarettes from where it's tucked behind a post, she pulls one out. "Of course I did. Her money makes her blind. What makes her so special, considering she has to live here? Does she think she has a lease on all the men?"

Zarina rolls with laughter. Shanti frowns, "Don't show me your ugly teeth. I don't like it."

Kusum goes out.

She walks southwards along the narrow lane. The rooms threaten to collapse on her at any moment. It's dark here even in daytime. Sunlight never wanders in, even by mistake. Piercing the darkness in the lane, Rohimon, the mad woman, appears suddenly. She cannot be considered anything but a skeleton. Her breasts and back are identical. She has a hole on her right cheek. Her nose has all but disappeared from a vicious illness. Two of her front teeth are missing. She lost them after getting beaten up by someone long ago. The muscles beneath her eyes are unnaturally swollen. Who knows when she last bathed. Watching Kusum, frowning and blinking, Rohimon says, "O Kusmi, where are you off to?"

Sidestepping Rohimon, Kusum says, "To call Babu. Shanti Buji's sent for him."

Rohimon chortles without reason. "Shanti's in demand these days, isn't she. Do you know I was also in demand once? A contractor, very rich you know, gave me a gold chain and earrings. He paid a lot of attention to me."

Her voice turns shrill. "So you see, Kusum *bibijaan*, no one here gets attention forever. Do you understand, you daughter of a whore, you cocksucker's maid?"

Kusum does not stop. She knows Rohimon will babble on now, telling Kusum stories of her glory days. She corners people whenever she can to boast of her heyday. She gets no business now. The ugly wound on her damaged nose oozes pus. She begs for a living, squatting at the entrance to the lane every evening and holding her hand out to anyone who passes by. Everyone knows that she doesn't usually buy food with the money she makes from begging; she buys hooch. She's out of control when drunk, hurling abuse at everyone in the world.

Barely has Kusum taken a couple of steps when Rohimon grabs her arm. Softly, she asks, "Will you lend me two taka?"

Kusum shakes her arm free. "Do you think I have money? And who'll give *you* a loan, anyway?"

Rohimon summons an invective to her lips. "Why, you bitch. You live in Shanti's room and you're telling me you can't steal any money? Don't you know how many people I lent money to once?"

Kusum doesn't wait any longer. She isn't enjoying having to stand next to this filthy, stinking Rohimon and having no choice but to see her ribs and her hideous nostrils. Kusum knows Rohimon is now going to knock on one door after another. If she gets some money, she'll use it for hooch at Chheru's shop and then pass out by the drain. Flies will buzz around her open mouth and the wound in her nose. Someone passing by might swear at her and kick her unconscious body closer to the drain.

Turning a corner, Kusum sees Piru and Parul playing with brick fragments on the broken expanse of concrete. Parul calls out to her, "*Ei* Kusmi, come play with us."

Piru is even younger than Kusum. Parul and Kusum are about the same age. Not even six months have passed since Piru came here. She was sold to Hiru Sardar for twenty-five taka. Parul came during the famine. Piru used to whine and weep by the well just the other day, talking of her parents and brothers and sisters. She no longer wept. Now she posed with the rest of them in the lane after dark.

Kusum pauses. "*Oi!* Wait till you hear what happened today."

Throwing the pieces up and catching them, Piru asks, "What happened?"

Kusum winks. "Shanti Buji taught Bokul Buji a lesson today."

Both Piru and Parul lower their arms to look at her curiously. Parul says, "Why, what happened?"

Kusum sneers. "Bokul Buji's man was gaping open-mouthed at Shanti Buji's body. So Bokul Buji lost her temper and attacked Shanti Buji. Now you tell me, who was to blame?"

Picking up the pieces of brick, Piru purses her lips. "I don't know who's to blame. Bokul Buji treated me to *tehari* once. She's very nice."

Parul cocks her head. "So what? Shanti Buji gave me a taka once."

She suddenly changes her tone. Curving her eyebrows in a world-weary way, she says, "Do you know, Kusum? I had five men yesterday. One of them has promised to take me to the movies."

Piru draws a line miserably on the mossy concrete with a brick fragment. "I hate having men. It hurts so much. What can

I do? Mashi beats me. I don't get food. I'll run away one day, you'll see."

Parul mimics her. "I'll run away. So easy! Hiru will rip your belly open first and throw you into the well."

Piru's eyes brim with tears. Suddenly she says, "Have you ever been on a launch, Kusum?"

Kusum smiles, gazing at a distant memory, "Once. I came to Dhaka on a launch."

Piru's eyes brighten. "It's such fun bathing in the river, no? And gathering the rice?"

Mashi comes down the stairs. All three stiffen. Piru looks the most afraid. As she passes, Mashi says, "*Oi* Parul, come to my room in a while."

At last, Kusum remembers she has come out in search of Babu. Doing errands for Shanti is usually to her benefit. She asks Parul, "Seen Babu anywhere?"

Getting to her feet and winding her coarse hair round her fingers, Parul says, "Babu's gone to the market."

Kusum goes back. All the doors are open now. The women are gathered in groups here and there. The older ones are chatting and picking lice, sitting on the crumbling steps with their legs stretched out. Kusum goes straight to Phulmoti's room.

Phulmoti is washing her baby's clothes with water drawn from the well. Her room can hardly be called a room. It consists of two expanses of cane strips woven together, propped up against dilapidated walls, and a sheet of tin. The floor is earthen. She used to live in a better room earlier. Her customers dwindled after she had a child. It's only recently that she has been getting a client or two. When she has a customer, Phulmoti wraps her baby in a sheet and leaves her with Sakina's grandmother in the other room. Now she calls out to Kusum, "O Kusum, hold the baby for a bit? I'll just wash these."

Phulmoti's baby is lying abandoned on a torn mat on the wet floor, screaming. Taking the baby in her arms, Kusum is startled. "O *bu*, your baby's skin is hot. Has she got a fever?"

Soaking the clothes in a little water and then rinsing them, Phulmoti looks at Kusum dismally. In a dejected voice, she says, "Yes. She's caught a cold. Cried all night. Wish I could massage her chest with some oil. But who's going to give me any? I'll go to the doctor this evening."

Putting the bedclothes up to dry on a line, Phulmoti returns. "Even those homoeopathy pills cost four taka. Tell me what to do."

Kusum says wisely, "All you need to do is get a few customers. That will pay for the medicine."

Phulmoti does not answer. She holds her baby to her breast for a feed. Kusum feels a strange sensation. A dim, distant memory . . . somewhere in the recesses of her mind. Her mother used to feed Kusum's little brother exactly this way. She feels a jolt. Looking at Phulmoti's scrawny worm-like baby, she tells herself, *no, I must never become a mother.* Like everyone else here, Kusum too knows what a crime it is to be the mother of a child in this brothel.

Many of the women are done with their morning chores and are lighting their stoves. The spaces beneath the rickety beds are packed with blackened and dented enamel pots, pans with broken handles, plates, discoloured tins of spices, oil and salt. Some have kerosene stoves, some have clay ovens. Thika Mashi has done the shopping and delivered everyone's orders. A slice of pumpkin here, a collapsed, soggy eggplant there. Some have a small piece of fish. For some of the women, though, it's fatty mutton and hilsa bought by Babu in Thataribazar.

Jahanara has risen late. Her room can only be described as elegant. So is Jahanara herself. And why shouldn't she be? How many of the women hereabouts have a body as flawlessly lovely as hers? Leave alone this brothel, which other woman in any brothel possesses a body as enticing as hers? The women who've entered the business without getting licences cannot match up to Jahanara. She can become a movie star right now if she so desires. She occupies a room on the first floor, near the head of the stairs. Although the plaster is flaking off its walls, the peeling floor is spotlessly clean. Jahanara has it swabbed twice a day. She has a part-time maid who cleans, washes her clothes, brings her water to bathe. Jahanara does not cook. All three of her meals come from the restaurant.

She has woken up a short while ago and smoked her way through four cigarettes in bed. She is relaxing as she watches the patch of sunshine on the wall next door through the half-yard-wide window with its broken bars. There is a giant painting of a nude on Jahanara's wall. Behind the figure is a hint of a blue ocean. Jahanara has never seen the ocean. The person who gave her the painting told her it was the sea. In moments of leisure, Jahanara has thought a lot about the way the sea looks. She has not been able to visualise it. All she can see in her mind's eye is the ugly, peeling wall next door that's visible through the window with the broken bars, and the thin segment of sky above the roof. She finds the voluptuous woman in the painting much more familiar. It makes her laugh too. She enters her body in a competition with the woman's.

Jahanara gets out of bed. Taking the bottle of liquor from the niche in the wall, she puts it away beneath her cot. Then she makes her bed herself, patting the delicate patterned sheets into place. Thika Mashi has already delivered the water in two buckets outside her door. Jahanara goes back into her room after a wash, shutting the door. Sounds of a commotion, screams and snatches of arguments, are floating upstairs.

Moyna pushes the door open and enters. The middle-aged Moyna has brought parathas and meat for Jahanara from the restaurant. Putting the breakfast plate and bowl down on a stool, Moyna says, "Give me the kettle, *bu*. I'll get your tea while you eat."

Moyna picks the kettle up from a corner of the room and leaves.

She has given up the trade now. Every evening, she sets up shop in the lane, selling *telebhaja*, chickpeas and eggs, which she prepares on a portable stove. By day, she works as a part-time maid for Jahanara, who is not only generous but also has a soft spot for Moyna. Sometimes she parts with some of the foreign liquor gifted by a rich customer. From time to time, she even tips Moyna, over and above her salary. A few days ago, she gave her a nylon sari. Of course, there's another reason for her treating Moyna so well. Jahanara gets terrible headaches sometimes. All the girls here suffer from headaches in varying degrees. They buy

Codopyrin tablets from Mannan's shop. But Jahanara's case is different. She is transformed when her headaches strike, her sophisticated ways forgotten. She screams, throwing her pillow and sheets away, smashing bottles, hurling obscene abuse at everyone in the world. No one can appear in Jahanara's presence when this happens. She physically attacks anyone she sees. Jahanara smashes her head against the wall, her forehead swelling. Moyna is the only one who can go up to Jahanara, smothering her in her arms and putting her to bed. Jahanara scratches, bites and kicks, trying to overcome Moyna, showering curses. "Get away, you whores. I'll kill the lot of you. I'll burn the house down."

Being beaten up doesn't bother Moyna. Forcing Jahanara's mouth open, she inserts two tablets of Sonaril with some water. Jahanara rolls around on the bed for a bit before quietening down. The flow of invectives ebbs. Moyna loosens Jahanara's bra, undoes the strings of her petticoat too, saying tenderly, "It'll be alright, everything will be alright. A rich man will marry you and take you away one day. You'll have children. A happy family."

Jahanara falls asleep to Moyna's murmurs, her eyes glazed. She holds on to Moyna's hand even in her sleep. She forgets that once, during a bout of this illness, she had thrown a bottle at Moyna's head. The wound on Moyna's forehead had taken a long time to heal. Now Jahanara remembers what happened last night. She had a peculiar customer. An educated, well-bred gentleman. Of course, most of Jahanara's customers are educated and well-bred. She no longer lines up for clients in the lane. Kanchan and Moyna escort them to her. The man last night had never been to Jahanara's room before. Moyna had fixed the rate before informing Jahanara. Jahanara had only asked, "What sort of man? I hope he has enough money."

Moyna had smiled. "Your fragrance has spread throughout the city, *buji*. People know your worth. Do you think everyone can come to your door? He's tipped me in advance."

Moyna had left after bringing the man to her. She didn't have a moment. This was when she ran her shop. Dressed in a pyjama and kurta, the man had glanced at the painting. Jahanara was sizing him up. By now, she can tell at first glance whether a customer is a regular or a newcomer. New customers have a tentative, embarrassed air. Jahanara no longer grants additional demands. In fact, she prefers to tease them. But the man yesterday had been quite different. He had stared unabashedly at the painting of the unclothed foreign woman on the wall. His expression had not suggested the impatience of a hungry man. On the contrary, after taking in the image with some amusement, and then running his eye over photographs of Jahanara in different poses on the wall, he had looked at her directly. "You're Jahanara?"

She had replied sarcastically, "Do you think you're in the wrong room?"

"No, I've heard a lot about you."

Jahanara had emitted a commercially seductive laugh. "And now you're here to see me in person? Do you know how much I charge?"

"I do. Fifty taka."

Taking his wallet out of his pocket, he had tossed a reddish fifty-taka note at Jahanara.

She had felt a surge of anger. Still, picking up the note with businesslike wariness, she had said, "Sit down."

He didn't seem to have heard her. He had walked around Jahanara's room, examining it. Suddenly he had asked, "Where are you from?"

Jahanara had lost her temper. "I don't have time for all this shit. Get started on what you're here for. I have other customers waiting."

The man had been unmoved. Sitting on Jahanara's bed, he had lit a cigarette and had then decided to offer her one too. She had lit up without hesitation, sitting down next to him. She was beginning to get angry at his disinterest. He wasn't impotent, was he? Many impotent men come here to have their climaxes simply by looking at shapely women's bodies. The girls don't care. So long as they're paid. They laugh amongst themselves the next day. Someone might say in a low voice when such a man is leaving, "Go do the hijra dance at Chheru's. What do you visit women for?"

The warmth of Jahanara's thighs was pressed on his. She dressed in only a thin sari in the evening, without a petticoat. No blouse. Satin bras bought at the biggest shop in town.

The man had turned to look at her. Exhaling smoke, he had smiled faintly. "You love all this, don't you?"

Jahanara had begun to hiss in rage. She wasn't as greedy as one of those women who only wanted the money. Fetching the fifty-taka note, she had tossed it at the man. "Fucking swine. You want to see a whore? Are we creatures in a zoo, you son of a bitch?"

Finally, the man had smiled broadly. "So you have a temper. But then that's because you're well-off. Would you have been able to throw that money at me if you'd been starving?"

Jahanara had been so surprised she had forgotten her rage. What sort of a man was this? Was he visiting a whore just for conversation? He wasn't even looking at her priceless, intoxicating body. Jahanara had started her seduction. Pressing the weight of her body against his, she had put her arms around him. "Shall we have a drink? I can't drink hooch though. Nothing but *bilati*."

The man had finished his cigarette. Fishing some money out of his pocket, he had held it out to her. "Get some."

Taking the money, Jahanara had gone out to the veranda, calling Moyna from the top of the stairs. Giving her the money and ordering a bottle of foreign liquor, she had gone back inside. The man had stubbed out the butt of his first cigarette on the floor with his heel and lit another.

The fifty-taka note was lying where Jahanara had flung it. He hadn't taken it back. Jahanara had picked it up again. Summoning a tender smile to her face, she said, "Are you new here?"

Gazing at her absently, the man had said, "Hmm."

"Are you married?"

"No."

"Do you have your own business?"

"No."

"Are you from the movies?"

"No."

"Now I see. You're here to paint."

"Not that, either."

"Why don't you come to bed then?"

The man had smiled strangely. "So many people come to your bed. What's the hurry?"

Jahanara had flared up again. "Our time is valuable."

"I know that. Tell me, Jahanara . . . You *are* Jahanara, aren't you? Do you consider yourself happy?"

Moyna had knocked on the door. "Here's your bottle, *buji*."

Jahanara had opened the door to take it. Throwing a look at the man out of the corner of her eye, she had handed a ten-taka note to Moyna. "How can we drink without some snacks? Get us some *sheek* kabab. Be quick about it. Tell Kanchan if you're busy."

Placing an arm on the door, Jahanara had stretched lusciously and smiled, "Well, lover boy? Are you just going to gape like a hero in a movie? Is the bottle all your heart wants?"

Blowing smoke towards the ceiling, the man had said, "Shut the door and come here."

Jahanara had smiled to herself. "Now you're talking, my boy. What were you playing all those tricks for?"

A bunch of incense sticks was burning on a shelf. The fragrant blue smoke brought the commercial sophistication of a welder's shop to the shabby room. Jahanara had sprinkled a few more drops of the water blessed at the Pirjangi shrine from the bottle she kept in a niche in the wall. Then she had returned to the man. She was beginning to get curious about him. She had seen all sorts of men. There had been no dearth of customers from the time she had started out in this business on the river bank. Jahanara didn't think of them as distinct individuals. She couldn't tell them apart.

The man had uncorked the bottle himself. Pouring a little into a glass, he had asked hesitantly, "No soda?"

Jahanara had gone off into peals of laughter. Part of her sari had fallen off her breasts. The man had stopped after a momentary glance at Jahanara's shapely breasts, her stomach, the delicate smoothness above her navel. "What are you laughing at?"

Jahanara had laughed even louder. Still laughing, she had said, "You're used to such fine ways of drinking. What have you come to our brothel for, *miah*? I've heard the ladies and gentlemen in your clubs and hotels have their drinks with soda and ice and dance with their arms around each other. This man's wife with that woman's husband. And he, with the other man's wife. You people have the best lives. No one calls your wives whores. You don't have to run around for licences."

Jahanara's eyes had begun to blaze. The man had laughed. "You know so many things."

Jahanara had stopped laughing. Snatching the bottle from the man's hand, she had filled their glasses. Offering one of them to the man, she had said, "Here's your drink. Don't waste my time with your shit. My regular customer will be coming tonight."

The man had raised his glass to his lips.

Moyna had knocked on the door again. "Here you are, *bu*. Your *sheek* kabab."

Slipping the packet through the half-opened door, Moyna had left. Jahanara had fetched the packet, still holding her glass. She had not restored her sari to the position where it covered her black-brassiered breasts. The end of her sari trailing on the floor, she had been sitting next to the man, holding him like a purring cat, rubbing his foot with hers to warm him.

Putting a piece of kabab in his mouth, the man had said, "You didn't tell me whether you're happy, Jahanara."

Jahanara had smiled with moist lips. "Yes, I'm quite happy."

Her eyes were touched by an euphoric intoxication now. The wariness in the lines on her face had softened. The man was slowly sipping his half-filled glass. He had not seemed in any hurry, as though he would be with Jahanara all night. Looking at her, he had continued, "But you'll grow old one day. You'll have no money then."

Jahanara had jerked upright. Her eyes inflamed with rage, she had burst out, "Why, you son of a bitch! Why should I not have money? Don't you know I have two liquor shops? I can start my own house if I want to. I can hire two dozen whores of my own. There's enough of them out there to bite, if I dangle the bait."

The man was looking at Jahanara, untroubled. She had refilled her glass. Holding it in one hand, she had suddenly wrapped her arms around him again and asked, sarcastically amorous, "You're so worried about me, are you planning to marry me and take me home?"

Evading the question, the man had said, "What if you get a bad disease, Jahanara? What will happen then?"

Jahanara's alcohol high had left her in an instant. Exploding in anger, she had slapped the man resoundingly. And then she had yelled, at the top of her voice, "Son of a bitch. May your family be fucked till they die. You swine, you think you can curse me just because you bought me a bottle of booze?"

The man hadn't flown into a temper at being slapped by Jahanara. His eyes had held amusement. Jahanara was on her feet in rage and agitation. She was no longer drunk. She was positively suspicious of this incomprehensible man. What was he up to?

He hadn't been sent by an enemy of hers, had he? Entirely possible, you never knew hereabouts. Gathering the end of her sari from the floor and wrapping it round her waist, Jahanara had gone on a rampage. She had shoved the man off the bed with both her hands and had begun to rant like a cantankerous whore, "Get out of my room at once, you bastard! Right now! If you don't, I'll get Kanchan to stick a knife in your stomach."

Unmoved till then, the man had finally been a little shaken by Jahanara's wrath. Slipping his feet into his sandals, he had said calmly, "Very well, I'm going. I'll be back, Jahanara."

He had indeed been about to leave. Jahanara had clutched his kurta from the back. "You'll be back? What for, you fucker? Jahanara spits on men who're cold-blooded snakes."

The man had stopped for a moment. "What do you think of a man as, Jahanara?"

Jahanara had loosened her hold on his kurta and spat on the floor. "I consider them dogs. Do you get me, you dog-breed? Now, disappear!"

Jahanara had virtually pushed the man out and slammed the door behind him. To tell the truth, he seemed to have poured a bucket of ice-cold water in Jahanara's room at the very beginning of her working hours. She was haunted constantly by a question and a sense of guilt. Her favourite regular customer, the young police officer, had turned up later. He had asked, "What is it, Janu? What's wrong with you today? You don't look fresh."

Jahanara had busied herself like a competent shopkeeper.
Undulating her body, she had taken a sip of her drink and smiled.
"A fox got into your darling's room today. I scared him away."

Lapping at her body with his eyes as though they were his
tongue, the police officer had softened like a dog given meat.
"Really? Old or new?"

Jahanara's attention is on important customers. She owns two
unlicensed liquor stores. It's thanks to the blessings of customers
like these that she doesn't get into trouble. Devoting herself to
her current customer, Jahanara had dismissed the whole thing.
"Forget it. He was a woman, not a man. Can't get it up, came to
rent a fuck."

After her regular customer had left, Jahanara had sent for
Moyna and Kanchan, questioning them at length about the man.
She had also warned both of them not to cut deals with customers
they knew nothing about. You never knew what some people
could be up to.

Moyna brings the kettle with tea in it. Removing the paper
plug from the spout, she says, "What's this, *bu*? You're still sitting
there with your breakfast. You're not sick, are you?"

Shaking off her worries from the previous night, Jahanara
returns to the present at once. Pouring some tea into a glass for
her, Moyna says, "Have your breakfast. I'll sweep the room.
Mashi's on her way to see you."

Her mouth full of paratha and gosht, Jahanara raises her eye-
brow questioningly. "What for? What does Mashi want?"

Running the broom across the floor swiftly, Moyna answers,
"What do you suppose? To settle the quarrel. Bokul and Shanti

fought today. Now Shanti's gone and thrown Bokul's clothes into the well."

"Why?"

"What else but a fight over a man. They're both the same. Full of airs on new money. They pay their own rents. Their customers are climbing too, like floodwater."

Taking a tin of bidis from her waist where she has tucked it in, Moyna lights one.

Jahanara sips her tea lazily, gazing at the mid-day sunlight in the sliver of sky through the window with the broken bars. Disinterestedly, she asks, "What can I do about it?"

Moyna cups her face in her hand in a show of surprise. "What are you saying? How can you not know what's going on here?"

Setting her glass of tea down on the floor noisily, Jahanara lights a cigarette, saying in irritation, "Of course. I must pass judgment on who's slapped whom and who's spat on whom. That's my job. I hate all these things in this fucked up place."

Moyna smiles, showing her stained teeth. Sidling up to Jahanara, she says, lowering her voice, "It's not going to end here. Bokul sent for that goon Gedu. He's a favourite of hers. Gedu beat up Shanti. What could Mashi do? Shanti's like a mad dog now after being beaten up. She's threatening to stop Bokul from working here. She'll throw acid on her. What if the quarrel leads to a murder or something, won't the police descend on us?"

Jahanara flops down on her bed. "Moyna, you've forgotten this business now that you're no longer in it. Let there be a murder. When has the police ever visited Golapipatti to investigate murders?"

Moyna nods in agreement. Picking up her broom, she says, "But whatever you may say, *bu*, what's the point of quarrelling amongst ourselves? Everyone has to sell their body for a living. Best not to create unnecessary trouble."

Jahanara smiles but does not reply. She feels a little self-satisfaction. She knows Mashi may arrive soon, asking her to settle things. Jahanara won't remain silent then. Both the accuser and the defendant will be summoned to her room. She will scold both of them, like an impartial guardian. Then she will say, "It's fine if you're willing to live peacefully, else I'll have both of you out of here."

It's not just Jahanara but also all the others who know that she is capable of doing this. Everyone here listens to what Jahanara says. From cutthroat goons to powerful individuals, she has access to all of them. She's also on good terms with senior officers.

Kanchan comes up the stairs busily. His face is pockmarked. One of his eyes is missing. A rival had ripped it out once. There had been trouble over a woman. Kanchan no longer plays the role of a goon. He has started a small shop, besides earning renown as a pimp. Standing outside the door, he says, "Has Janu woken up, Moyna?"

Jahanara sits up in bed, "What is it, Kanchan?"

Kanchan says with a smile, "I have news. Big news."

Throwing her broom aside, Moyna straightens eagerly. A shadow of concern flits across Jahanara's face. Now what? There's always something happening here. Has Bokul and Shanti's quarrel turned worse?

Jahanara says, "Come in. Don't stand there grinning."

Kanchan enters and sits on Jahanara's bed. Jahanara says, "Get two cups of tea, Moyna."

Picking the kettle up, Moyna pauses for a moment. Jahanara glares at her. "What are you gaping at, you hag? Didn't I tell you to get some tea?"

Moyna leaves with a sour expression, grumbling so that both of them can hear, "Moyna for work and Kanchan for tea."

Jahanara ignores her. She knows Kanchan and Moyna fight for her attention.

Kanchan says, "Give me a cigarette, Janu."

Jahanara holds her packet out to him. Lighting up, Kanchan scrunches his face and smiles, "You'll be smoking expensive cigarettes today."

Jahanara looks at him squarely. "Spell it out. What are you keeping from me?"

Kanchan says with a wink, "A shaheb from Gulshan has sent word."

Jahanara sits up in excitement. "Which car, the blue one or the white?"

"The one with the blue car. You have to go there."

"When?"

"At eleven tonight."

"Where? Hotel or home?"

"Home. I think it's for a friend. They don't tell me everything."

"How much have you settled at?"

"How much do you suppose? The same as last time."

Jahanara looks sharply at Kanchan. "Don't try to be smart, Kanchan. What's your commission?"

Kanchan curls his lips in reckless contempt. "Don't you give me all that, Janu. Kanchan isn't dealing in women for the first time. I can send Bokul instead of you."

Jahanara changes her expression. She wants to stay in Kanchan's good books. No one else could have got her such a big customer. She knows all these pimps inside out.

No one is reliable when it comes to money. Kanchan is temperamental. But still, he is more or less trustworthy. Besides, he has struck up a friendship with Jahanara over their long association. Not that friendships last very long here, because self-interest comes first.

Moyna brings the tea. Rinsing the glasses and pouring tea into two of them, she says, "I'm going to the market. I'll swab the floor and wash your clothes when I'm back. I brought you the water for your bath."

Jahanara calls her back when she's at the door. "*Oi* Moyna, have a cigarette before you go."

Passing the lit cigarette between her fingers to Moyna, Jahanara picks up her glass of tea. After Moyna leaves, she looks at Kanchan, a smile appearing on her face, and asks, "A friend of the shaheb's? Or is it a bribe?"

Sipping his tea, Kanchan narrows his eyes and smiles. "I think it's a bribe. This is what the world is like, everyone's trying to exploit someone. The shaheb is chasing a big contract. He's offering women as bribes. How much will you and I make, anyway? It's the fucking big people who'll lap up the cream."

Jahanara giggles, letting herself fall on Kanchan. Slapping his thigh lightly, she says, "If it's such a big *contaact*, why doesn't he offer his daughter and wife as bribes? Won't cost him, either. His wife and children live in a palace, move around in cars. You know what I think, Kanchan?"

Holding his derisive smile on his lips, Kanchan says, "Out with it."

Jahanara bites her lip for a moment. Then she says, her voice brimming with hate, "I wish I could throw acid on that bastard's woman's beautiful body and let it burn."

Putting his glass of tea on the floor, Kanchan rises to his feet. "Forget these lousy ideas. It's because they exist that whores like you can ride in cars and drink for *feeree* and charge high rates. And we make some money too."

Jahanara shouts back, "Don't tell me all this. How will they buy their *contaacts* without us? This deal will make me rich, I'll build a new house, buy a car, go abroad with my family. Would any of it be possible without the whores of Golapipatti?"

Kanchan is in a hurry to leave. But still he stops. "Look, Jani. You're talking too much these days. Don't you know you can get educated, well-bred whores in the city now? They live with their families and they're in the business too. It's only this shaheb from Gulshan who sends for women from Golapipatti."

Jahanara erupts violently, "Shut up, you swine! I've seen enough of those well-bred women. They don't know the *tiricks* we do. Go downstairs, you'll find an educated wife from a good family. The Punjabi military raped both her and her reputation. How many customers does she get every night?"

Kanchan's expression changes. "Are you talking of Yasmin? Is she even a woman? A plank of wood."

Jahanara snorts. "Well then? Is it so easy to be a prostitute?"

Kanchan doesn't stay any longer. Before leaving, he says, "Practise your English. The shahebs often want to hear the Golapipatti women address them as 'darling.'"

TWO

It's still quite bright outside. But darkness has descended within the lane. Sunlight has withdrawn quite some time ago after bouncing off the buildings on either side. The girls are busy in their rooms. A crowd has started gathering at Chheru's shop. Another hooch shop has also opened next door. Laying out skewers of *sheek* kabab on their clay ovens, the soot-covered boys are keeping an eye on the entrance to the lane in expectation of customers. Kerosene lamps are being lit in every room. Many of the girls have dressed up and taken their places in the lane. Kusum goes up to Yasmin's room and stops outside the door. Two other girls share the room with Yasmin. Marjina and Huree, the other occupants of the nine-foot-by-twelve-foot room, have dolled up and gone out.

Yasmin is sitting on her cot, her feet dangling. Kusum says hesitantly from the door, "*Buji*, can you give me a little *chhono?*" Yasmin turns towards the door. "Who's that? Kusum? What do you want?"

Kusum has indeed bathed today. Asking Shanti and not Zarina for some soap, she has washed her hair and her clothes. But her starving face looks lacklustre. Kusum says again hesitantly, "A little *chhono.*"

Yasmin gets up. "I don't have any snow or powder, Kusum. Marjina or Huree might have some. They aren't in."

Looking around apprehensively, Kusum says, "Don't tell them, *buji*. Just show me where it is, I'll take a little with my fingers."

Lowering her eyes, she continues, "Kalu will kill me if I don't get a customer tonight. I won't get to eat. I can't sleep nights from hunger."

Incense sticks are glowing in the room. All the girls light them when evening falls. They also sprinkle on themselves the sacred water from the shrine next to the High Court. All of them believe this will improve their business and protect them from illness. Yasmin alone doesn't do it. Many of her habits are out of tune with the girls in this brothel. She's different. Many of the people here avoid her. Her eyes fixed on Kusum's drawn, miserable expression, Yasmin rises to her feet. Marjina locks her cosmetics away in a trunk. Huree's powder and kohl are in a paper box beneath her bed. Pulling it out, Yasmin says, "Take what you need quickly. Huree will create a scene if she sees."

As Kusum is about to leave, having swiftly grabbed a fistful of power and some kohl with her fingertips, Huree appears at the door. Sizing up the situation in a moment, she pounces on Kusum. "You bitch, you couldn't find someone else to steal from? How dare you!"

Huree shakes Kusum's soaped-and-cleaned hair loose from her ponytail. Yasmin protests, "Why do you have to do this, Huree! All she's taken is a little powder. You can afford it, she can't."

Huree stops raining blows and kicks on Kusum and charges towards Yasmin. "Oh, so much love! If you're so sympathetic, why can't you give her some of your own? Go flaunt your elegance in your own posh neighbourhood. In front of those who drove you out to this place."

She turns to Kusum again in great fury. "You thieving bitch, what else have you stolen from me all these days?"

Cowering under her blows, Kusum says, "I won't do it again, *bu*. Let me go."

Huree shoves Kusum out of the room. Kusum falls on the uneven ground outside under the impetus of Huree's strength. The kohl on her fingers is smeared all over her face. Her freshly washed clothes are caked with mud. Kusum gets to her feet. Blood is trickling from lips cut open by a corner of a brick. She throws a malevolent glance at Huree before walking away.

As Huree rearranges her box of cosmetics, all her rage bears down on Yasmin. It's all the doing of this evil bitch. Behaves like an empress. Can't even afford to cook every afternoon. Eats with Marjina when she can. Survives on tea and biscuits most other days. Or even tea alone. And that Marjina is in awe of her. Says she's not like us, she's an educated woman, after all. Marjina often shares her meal with Yasmin. Huree gets angry. In her head, she says, *what do you give yourself all those airs for, you bitch? Since you're doing business here, you're just like the rest of us.* But no, she makes Thika Mashi get her the newspaper to read. When Marjina and Huree flop down on the cot every afternoon to pick lice and discuss movies, Yasmin lies in bed reading second-hand English novels. Most evenings, she doesn't line up in the lane, though sometimes she goes every day. She earns quite well when she does that. That's when she pays the rent she owes. Then something happens to her and she stays in bed all day. Instead of soliciting customers in the lane, she slumps down by the draw-well without speaking to anyone.

Standing upright, Huree puts her hands on her hips and looks at Yasmin with narrowed eyes. "I'm warning you not to encourage thieves."

Yasmin is silent. She does not speak. Huree continues, "If you feel so much for her, buy her things with your own money."

Marjina comes to the door with a customer. "Outside, you two. I've got someone."

Huree goes off to the lane sulkily to snare customers. Yasmin goes out of the room. A single room, a single bed. It has to be vacated for whoever gets a customer. There's a furore when everyone has a customer at the same time.

Yasmin walks along the lane slowly. A man asks, "Want a customer?"

She hears but pays no attention. The lane is vibrant now. People everywhere and the air thick with bargaining, laughter and solicitation. Kusum is waiting too, having washed her face and hands. Piru and Parul stand next to her. They describe their bodies and skills in a dull whine, to broadcast their appeal. The twelve-year-old Piru is tugging at a middle-aged man's shirt, pleading with him to rent her body.

Parul is chasing a youngish fop. She keeps embracing his flashily-belted waist from the back. He shakes her off, responding to Zarina's signals over on the other side.

Kusum has got hold of a man. They've settled on a price of five taka. She's leading him to her room like a victorious queen. Yasmin realises the man can claim to be as old as Kusum's father. She has learnt of the diversity and perversion in male tastes after getting here. Which is why even Piru finds customers, why she can get busy looking for customers. Not getting a customer means heartless humiliation at the owner's hands. On top of which there's fear and hunger—the same hunger which most of the girls here have fallen victim to and ended up, willingly or unwillingly, as nothing but bodies in the decrepit rooms in this lane where no sunlight or air gets in, eaten away by commercial deals every day, like slaves traded thousands of years ago, amidst cruel, ruthless, inhuman behaviour, surviving as creatures of the night.

Yasmin sits down in the darkness on the slimy bricks by the well. The aroma of *telebhaja* and fried spices from Moyna's roadside shop across the lane is mingling with the stench of garbage rotting in the drain, the vapid odour of putrid water in the well and the acidic tang of hooch. The neighbourhood is now a world of sounds and smells. A world of hoodlums, pimps, screams, tears, quarrels, coarse laughter, and bestiality. Sometimes Yasmin feels herself choking at this hour. It's as though a wild animal is mangling the world like a plaything. Yasmin wants to throttle herself then. She wishes she could pray to an unseen force to turn her into an inanimate object with no sensations, or at least into a blind beast. She had let herself be driven out to this place so she could turn blind. Why then does her conscience rise in revolt?

People are going up and down the stairs. Mashi comes downstairs. Spotting Yasmin in the darkness, she pauses. Yasmin can sense her corpulent form even without any light. She can tell that one of Mashi's eyes, which is made of stone, is turned towards her, lifeless and unmoving. Leaning forward, Mashi puts her hand on her hip and asks, "Who's that?"

Yasmin does not answer.

Mashi walks towards her. "Who are you? Why don't you answer?"

The door to Sakina's room is open. Her aged grandmother has gathered her grandchildren around herself. She has put a pot of rice to boil on the stove. The old woman has partitioned the room with straw mats strung from the ceiling. She sits on one side with her grandchildren in the evening. Her daughters sell their bodies on the other side. A faint beam of light from their room has fallen on Yasmin's untied hair and right cheek. Identifying her in this low illumination, Mashi straightens up and says, "So it's you. How come you're not looking for customers?"

Yasmin looks away. "I don't feel like it today."

Mashi is furious. "Look, girl, don't start acting like a lady. You have to pay my rent. I have to explain the accounts to Kazi Shaheb, don't I? When you came, I gave you a room at once, no questions asked. I could have two other girls in the room if you left."

Yasmin whips around to face her. "Go away, Mashi. I'm not in the mood. Does your rent ever remain unpaid? Even if it's overdue for a week, I pay it at once."

Mashi softens. Like the others, she too treats Yasmin differently from everyone else. Yasmin is quite attractive, but for some reason, none of her customers goes back to her a second time. Even after three years, she doesn't have a single regular customer. Yasmin isn't exactly the first girl from a well-bred family Mashi has seen here, but she's very unusual. Stiff, wooden. Mashi says, "Not feeling well? Why not get a tablet from Mannan's shop?"

Suddenly Yasmin asks, "Mashi, did you have parents?"

Mashi smiles in the darkness. "Listen to her. Can anyone be born without parents? Aren't you supposed to be educated? How can you ask such an idiotic question?"

Yasmin laughs loudly. "You claim to have been in the trade since you were sixteen. But you must have had parents and a home before that."

Mashi melts. "Get me the stool from the staircase there, let me sit down. This rheumatism won't let me stand."

Yasmin gets up to fetch the stool. Mashi sits down in silence. This unusual woman asks her strange questions sometimes, shaking her very foundations. Everyone else here is deferential to Mashi, though. To them, Mashi is a fat woman. Mashi was once a prostitute with a formidable reputation. Mashi means a flinty landlady, who still spends the night sometimes with the ferocious young gangster Saif. She gets stoned on opium. She teaches the women vulgar gestures and lewd tricks to snare customers. She buys girls at prices ranging from ten taka to seven hundred and puts them in the trade. Nobody thinks of her in any other way.

Yasmin asks again, "Aren't you going to answer, Mashi?"

Mashi lights a cigarette in the darkness. Her pockmarked face and stone eye flash for a moment in the flare of the match before being lost to the darkness. Taking a drag of her cigarette, Mashi says, "Do you really think I remember all this!"

"You really don't remember? What was your name, Mashi?"

"What a mad girl you are! This is your time for getting customers, not for asking about my life."

Mashi pauses. Then she says, "Baba used to call me Saraswati. Ma called me Sati. As chaste as Sati is what I am today."

Yasmin becomes animated. "Everyone has a name, isn't that so, Mashi?"

"Of course. An address too. And then they are swept away somewhere else. Otherwise I would have remained the daughter of a Brahmin. He got me married at the age of nine."

Mashi loses herself in a sea of memories. The nine-year-old bride became a widow before the year was out. Her father had a middling income. They used to live in a village near Dhaka. The little widowed girl grew up swimming in the pond, gathering flowers for her father's puja and playing with her dolls. Of course, she was forbidden to eat meat or fish and had to fast regularly in keeping with the rituals of widowhood.

Her mother would grieve, "My Sati has nothing but bad luck."

Sati had no idea what bad luck meant. She learnt it later, when puberty suddenly overflowed the banks of her body one day, like the Dhaleshwari river in the monsoon. Her mother would revile her bitterly, "What a body you've developed. I can't sleep at night out of worry. Turn your mind to religion, start fasting."

Sati didn't care for all this. The stormy wind blowing in from the river would unsettle her. She would burn with envy at the sight of her married sisters and cousins and girls of her age from the village. It was those wild winds that broke her. Her voluptuous, seductive figure caught the eye of her elder sister's husband. It didn't stay under wraps. One day, her father locked her up and thrashed her unmercifully.

Her enraged mother cursed, "Tie a rock to your neck and drown yourself. Why can't you die!"

After arousing a new desire in his sister-in-law's body and heart, her sister's husband left for his workplace in Barisal with his family. The widowed Sati suffered in her separation and her humiliation. The second honey-gatherer was not long in arriving. The Brahmin's daughter eloped with a lower-caste young man from the village, giving up her links to her clan. And then . . .

Yasmin asks, "And then?"

Mashi seems to have forgotten herself as she tells her story, as though she does not belong to this neighbourhood. Startled by Yasmin's question, she says, "What do you suppose? The son of a bitch abandoned me and ran away one day. So I came here . . . "

Mashi smokes in silence.

Yasmin says, "But the Hindu Marriage Law had been passed by then."

Mashi answers wistfully, "So what? It wasn't the practice yet."

After a moment's silence Mashi resumes, "Once, you know—I used to live in Sachi port back then—a Hindu widow from an aristocratic family came into the business. You should have seen how fair she was, how beautiful. No one had brought her there, she signed up on her own and moved in. She never took Hindu customers. She would say, 'After I die, I don't want to be reborn as a woman in a Hindu family. I'll have to starve to death if I become a widow.'"

Somebody rushes up to them. It's Moyna, notes Yasmin. Moyna starts howling when she sees Mashi, "O Mashi, come quick! Someone's about to be killed."

Mashi jumps to her feet. "What is it, Moyna? What's the matter?"

Moyna says agitatedly, "Come and see for yourself. Bokul got someone for twenty taka, double her rate. Bokul was dancing with joy at getting twenty as she took her man in and locked the door. The bastard didn't want to do anything. He had a long whip in his pocket. He stripped Bokul and whipped her all over, every inch of her body."

An unperturbed Mashi says, "Is that all?"

An anxious Yasmin stands up. "What's all this, Mashi? Is he mad?"

Mashi sits down on her stool again. "Not mad at all. There are men who don't get aroused till they hurt women. Has he left, Moyna?"

Moyna warbles, "Yes he has. When Bokul started screaming, Shanti, Zari and the rest of them broke the door down and found wounds all over her body. The bastard saw his chance and escaped."

Mashi says calmly, "This sort of thing happens regularly. She'll be fine. The blood of a whore. No harm done."

Yasmin shifts uneasily. "Let me go see how she is, Mashi."

One side of the termite-ridden door of Bokul's room has collapsed. Yasmin shivers at the sight of Bokul's naked, unconscious form on the bed, lit by the reddish glow of the lamp. A wild animal seems to have sliced up her body with its claws. She is bleeding. A miserable Shanti is wiping her body with a rag. She doesn't look as though she had a violent quarrel with Bokul this morning. Yasmin tells Zarina, who's standing there, "Mannan should have Dettol in his shop. Get a bottle."

Bokul's clenched fist holds her customer's payment. Zarina prises a note out and leaves. The crowd gathered outside Bokul's door also thins. Everyone goes off to work. The women cannot waste time now. Each of them must get hold of nine or ten customers. The man who has done this to Bokul might be among them. No one remembers faces, especially new faces. But there's no choice. They need customers, they need money. Every night is valuable. The girls wait all day for night to fall. Especially the penniless among them. Those who don't get customers. Who don't get food. Who have to stomach their owners' kicks and punches. Who cannot save enough money to buy water for even one bath a month. The women return to their places in the lane with wan faces.

Zarina comes back with the Dettol. Taking the bottle, Shanti says, "Now that you're here, Yasmin Bu, let me go. I have a man in my room. Someone might lure him away."

Zarina turns towards the door too. "I have to go as well. Just got one customer tonight."

After they've left, Yasmin swabs Bokul's body with Dettol. Unfolding the bunched up sari, she spreads it over Bokul. Then she calls softly, "Bokul! *Ei* Bokul!"

The tumbledown room looks ghostly by the light of the lamp. The shadow cast by Bokul's supine body on the bamboo wall is immobile.

A faint voice emerges. "Give me some water, *bu*."

Pouring a glass of water from the pitcher, Yasmin holds it to Bokul's lips. The quarrelsome, brash, alluring Bokul is weeping. Yasmin consoles her sadly, "Don't cry, Bokul."

Now Bokul bursts into tears. "Oh, *bu*! What do these sons of pigs think we are? Don't we have the bodies of human beings? Hasn't Allah sent us to earth as humans?"

Putting the glass down, Yasmin levels a steady gaze at Bokul. She says, "Not humans. Women."

Bokul is suddenly wracked by some unknown sorrow. She sobs loudly now, her bloody, lacerated body still writhing in pain.

Yasmin leaves the room in silence. Like a helpless spirit imprisoned within the dirty, dilapidated, unhealthy confines of the room, Bokul's heartrending cries turn into the lament of the entire brothel and rise with a plaintive plea to some invisible controlling power.

Yasmin returns to her stool by the well.

Mashi has gone. Business is being conducted in every room, buying and selling.

Zarina is standing outside her room with a customer, banging on the door. Shanti is inside with a man. Zarina is screaming, "*Oi* Shanti! Come out, you bitch! How many taka is your customer paying for you to have to lock the door for so long? Come out, come out! My man is waiting."

Yasmin looks away. Shanti will emerge any moment now and abuse Zarina and her entire family all the way back to her ancestors. They may even get into a fight. Zarina, Shanti and Kusum share the same room, the same rickety bed, for their business. There is often a crisis. There's a big problem if all of them get customers at the same time. Allowing one of them to use the room first, the other two wait outside, hurrying the one within to vacate the room quickly, while holding their customers back with lewd jokes.

The sounds of Sakina's grandmother and the old woman's grandchildren reading their schoolbooks wafts out of their room. They study at the free primary school nearby.

Yasmin smiles. As if it's not two children aged seven and nine, but tomorrow's Kanchan or Kalu, Bokul or Zarina, who are aimlessly studying the alphabet. Their lives are different from those of others. Their grandmother is a madam in her own right. She's got her daughter and granddaughters to join the business. She tells the others proudly, "Do you suppose we drifted here from nowhere, like the rest of them? We've been here for four generations."

Maybe the hag has glorious dreams of her radiant seven-year-old granddaughter surpassing even Jahanara in beauty and seductive tricks. And that her nine-year-old grandson will be a powerful, invincible thug.

But what if it hadn't been this way? What would it have been like then? Yasmin loses herself in the darkness, gazing at the tiny patch of sky discernible around a solitary star. A little seven-year-old girl would be living, not in the messy environment of a whorehouse but in a healthy, happy household, swinging her feet as she studied under electric lights. She was not supposed to have been like Bokul, Shanti, Zarina or even Yasmin. Her father had a decent job. Never took a bribe in his life. Her mother never skipped the namaz. That girl would lower her head to her desk while studying and enter a different universe, like Alice did through the mirror. A universe of birds, flowers, rivers.

But little did she know how fragile the mirror was! One day it would be shattered by brutal and cruel carnivorous beasts. And, filled with hatred for the entire world, that girl would become Yasmin. A wayward soul in Golapipatti. A helpless spectator to the worst barbarity and savagery on earth. Burning day and night in the agony of repugnance for all humans. The distant stars are shining with a faint hint of light in the summer sky. Looking at them wistfully, Yasmin imagines she has been flung to earth from a world as far away as those stars, arriving in this dark place like a planet wrenched out of its orbit. Just like most of the women here have. Suddenly contempt flashes at the corner of Yasmin's mouth. How effortlessly all those people out there laugh, sleep, eat, point and judge. They are the ones who had given her a mouthful of a name. She recalls it, Birangona. Heroic woman.

Concealing the derision in their eyes and the revulsion on their lips behind a mask of pity, they had said, "You are a heroic woman." As though implying, "You're not like all other innocent women in society."

Yasmin feels a surge of anger within her. If only she could stand up to this rotting, corroded society like a real heroic woman! But she had failed. And the power of that hypocrisy had dragged her into this slime.

Someone seems to be dragging a body along the lane.

Rohimon can be heard, "You swine, you son of a whore, let go! Take your hands off me."

Then the sharp voice of Bachhir, the boy who works at Chheru's shop, "If I find you stealing again, I'll slit your throat and dump your body in the drain. You thieving bitch! You think you can just swipe your hooch?"

Someone passing by with quick footsteps asks, "What is it, Bachhir? Has the *maagi* stolen again?"

Throwing Rohimon to the ground, Bachhir complains in agitation, "This fucking bitch has nine lives, like a cat. Gets knocked around all day, still doesn't die. She's stolen today too. Pretends to be mad. Cunning as hell."

Rohimon snaps at him, "As if you're so pure, you son of a bitch! As if you don't steal the hooch yourself and sell it to the girls."

Bachhir aims a kick at Rohimon's frail ribs. "Shut up, you whore! Can't afford to buy food, begs for her liquor, just listen to her talk."

Shoving Rohimon against the wall, Bachhir leaves. She sobs loudly for some time, saying through her tears, "Every one of you is a son of a *khanki*. To hell with all of you!"

Her tears subside and her voice becomes sharper. "I want to see how long they can flaunt their bodies or drink *bilati* or dance with their lovers."

Rohimon continues whining. Her begging probably hasn't earned her anything today. She hasn't been able to drink herself into a stupor. She goes mad when she can't do that. Rohimon gets to her feet. She comes up to Yasmin, dragging her feet in the darkness, but recognising her in spite of it. Slumping to the ground, she wraps her arms around Yasmin's knees. "Will you lend me five taka, girl? I'll die if I don't have a drink."

Rohimon's breath carries the sour fume of cheap liquor. She is drunk. Yasmin extricates herself from Rohimon's grip. She says, "I have no money."

A stubborn Rohimon grabs Yasmin's leg again. "What do you mean? A full-bodied bitch with no money in the evening! Hand it over. I'll return it tomorrow."

Pushing Rohimon away, Yasmin stands up. "I've told you already, I have no money."

Rohimon flares up in rage. "Fine, if you don't want to, don't give me any. But don't you push me, you whore. Who do you think you are? You think anyone can be happy forever in a whorehouse? Not even a dog will look at you when you grow old. Your nose will rot away. You'll go mad and hang yourself or starve to death. No one will care."

Yasmin gets up to extricate herself from Rohimon's clutches. Where can she go? Not to her room. Marjina and Huree are doing their work. She has a headache. Yasmin often has these headaches after coming here. Like everyone else, she too takes Codopyrin tablets.

Yasmin goes up to Mannan's shop. It's full of customers. Everyone's buying things. Sprinkling water on the rows of paan laid out on a red cloth, Mannan smiles toothily, "What do you need, *bu?*"

Like the others, Mannan too is somewhat deferential to Yasmin. She tells him in a forlorn voice, "Give me a Codopyrin. I'll pay tomorrow."

Mannan doesn't usually give credit. He knows the girls here only too well. Once he lets them run up a tab, it will be impossible to get them to settle. Yasmin is the only exception. She always pays her dues. Handing over a tablet, Mannan says, "The payment for last week's pills is due too."

Yasmin nods. "I'll pay both this week."

The pills are birth-control pills, which everyone here has to buy at Mannan's shop. Even if they cannot afford food, they have to find the money for the pills. They are terrified of motherhood. Having children means a drop in business. Lower earnings. On top of which there's the responsibility of bringing the child up. Still, there are accidents. And the outcome is a curse.

As Yasmin is about to leave, Mannan says, "Not taking anyone to your room today?"

Yasmin does not reply. Serving a customer paan with deft hands, Mannan says, "I can see you're not in the mood."

On her way back, Yasmin hears Mannan tell someone, "Not surprising. She's an educated woman. Conceited. But a good soul."

The night deepens. The liveliness dissipates slowly. The crowds thin at Chheru's dive, which has been buzzing with customers all this while. Business subsides. Three or four drunks raise a commotion. Some of the women appear at Moyna's shop, buying whatever's left for their dinner. They have a hot meal just once a day—virtually no one has the time to cook at night. Some fill their bellies with leftovers from the afternoon and slump on their beds in sheer exhaustion. Three or four of them curl up in sleep in each of the cramped rooms. The old hag Golapjaan coughs continuously through the night. Sometimes the women are startled in their sleep by the sound of heavy footsteps in the lane. These people don't show up like everyday customers. They are special. Mashi goes to bed after everyone else. She sits on the stool outside Mannan's shop till late in the night, chatting with him. The tall, solitary streetlamps light up the midnight street outside. And in the lane, the night runs through the hours with some light, some darkness, some sleep, some wakefulness.

THREE

Piru is weeping in bed. Parul is asleep next to her, limbs splayed, mouth open. She's all over the place when she sleeps. Her legs are on Piru's body. They live in a room at the farthest end of the first floor. It's a tiny room. No window. The cement on the floor has come off almost entirely. The crumbling, exposed bricks on the wall do not look as though they were ever covered by a layer of plaster and paint. Large slabs fall off the roof frequently. Things get worse when it rains. Water drips in, flooding the room. Of course, every room gets its share of rain. But none of the other rooms is in as bad a shape as the ones at this end. Piru is afraid every time she enters. Still, they have to get several customers into this room every day. Piru does not keep the money the men pay her. She does not run an independent business. She gets her food in exchange for offering her body. A sari now and then. Just for this, she has to suffer terribly at her owner's hands. Hiru is their owner.

Hiru owns ten of the women here. Piru and two others occupy this room. Hiru has to pay a rent of fifty taka a day. That often leaves nothing by way of profits. He turns violent when that happens, abusing the girls in the filthiest of language, beating them up mercilessly. The twelve-year-old Piru suffers the lion's share of the thrashing. And gets the least to eat. Today, too, Piru didn't get a customer. She had hidden in the terrace. Hiru had found her and marched her off to Mashi, in whose presence he had given her a thrashing. No one had bothered. No one would raise a finger even if a pimp were to kill one of the women they own. That was the rule here. A furious Hiru had dragged Piru by her hair to Mashi and flung her on the ground. Delivering a hefty kick to her tiny chest, he had said, "Tell me what to do with her, Mashi. She was hiding on the roof instead of taking in customers."

Mashi had looked at Piru with a frown. "Well, you bitch, why were you hiding on the roof?"

Piru had not answered.

Hiru had begun to scream, "I paid a hundred for her in cash. You think money grows on trees! I'm paying through my nose for their clothes and food and room. And *maagi* goes into hiding. Fix her, Mashi."

Hiru had returned soon with a fat drunk. Giving Piru a shove, he said, "Take him to your room. I'll kill you if you run away again."

Piru had clung to a leg of Mashi's stool, refusing to move.

Hiru had shouted at her, "Are you going or not?"

Even Mashi had said, "Don't be stubborn, Piru. Take the man to your room."

Piru had suddenly burst into tears. "I can't. I'll die. Let me go, I beg of you."

Mashi had kicked her hard to loosen her grip on the stool. "No need for all this *nokhra*. If the other girls can do it, why can't you?"

Hiru had turned violent, landing one kick after another on Piru. "Let you go? Fuck you! Pay my money back first, you bitch."

Piru had writhed on the floor near Mashi's feet under Hiru's onslaught. Mashi had just sat there without moving a muscle. Finally Piru's little body had become motionless. Hiru had dumped her inert body in her room like the carcass of a dog. Then, leading the customer to the same room, he had taken a seat next to Mashi, smoking. Piru's groans were not audible there.

In the dark room, Piru moves Parul's legs off her body and sobs into her pillow. She is numb with pain. She had to take in four customers after Hiru's merciless beating. Hiru's customers were as cruel as him. They had torn her frail body apart like hungry beasts. It was almost as though Hiru had taught them to do this. One of them had bitten some flesh off her neck. Piru cannot take this anymore. She wants to die. But still she lives. During the day, she chats with girls her age about the experiences of the night. She plays marbles. Queues up for meals, plate in hand. Piru doesn't earn well. So she gets no food on her plate most days. Even when she does, it's just rice and daal, which does-n't assuage her hunger. She's so famished, her limbs throb in pain. The dirty, uneven lane undulates like a snake before her eyes.

Parul is asleep. She's not like Piru. Although she's about the same age, she has become wise to the ways of this whorehouse. She has great enthusiasm for enticing customers, though she has to work very hard at it. Still, she's eager to please them. She even gets tips for it, extra earnings. She uses it for snacks at Moyna's shop, and ribbons and hair-clips at Mannan's. She joins the older girls in listening to gossip about movie stars. She tells Piru, "I'm going to be like Jahanara Bu when I grow up. I'll go out in cars. Buy shops. Put my feet up and order others around."

Parul had come here during the famine. Her stepmother had sold her to a pimp. She had no fond memories of home. Ever since she could remember, all she'd got was her stepmother's hatred. Her father hadn't bothered about her. Whenever someone asks about him, Parul spits on the ground and says, "He was a swine."

Parul's father had died before the famine. He used to work as a labourer on people's farms. He didn't have any land of his own. Parul's stepmother had sold their ramshackle home during the famine. Then Parul had come to the city with her stepmother and several stepbrothers and stepsisters. After drifting from one place to another like flotsam, they had turned up at this horrible place. Parul's stepmother had gauged a price for the starving, exhausted girl. Enticing her with a meal at the *langarkhana*, her stepmother had sold her for just thirty taka. A pimp had bought the weary Parul. But she had no regrets. She had been delivered from the agony of starvation and the tyranny of her stepmother.

But Piru cannot be like Parul. As soon as she takes her humiliated, famished body to bed every night, her little heart is twisted with grief. What floats up in Piru's tears are images not of this filthy establishment but of a green village. After spending all afternoon diving and swimming in the river, Piru would gather a bundle of *koloi shaak* from the fields and return home, where her mother would be lighting the stove and putting a pot of rice on it.

Piru's family was not well off. Her father would work on other people's fields as a daily labourer during farming season. In the rainy season, he would catch fish in the river from a boat he shared with others. They had no land, no cattle. Piru's mother would husk and grind grain for rich landowners. Piru and her little brother Ali would wander around the village all day. A miserable life? Not at all. Lying on tattered sheets at night, she would listen to the drip-drip of the dew on the roof, the jackals howling in the potato fields. Listening closely despite the sound of torrential rain, she would hear sections of the river bank falling into the water. Piru would be terrified then. She would reach out for her mother, sobbing. Her mother would caress her, saying, "O Piru, Piru *re*, what is it? Are you afraid? Bad dream?"

Piru would put her arms around her mother and go back to sleep.

Parul turns on her side, hurling an obscenity at someone in her sleep. She has dreams of this place when asleep. Piru conjures up another dream through her tears. A small canal used to run in front of the house she had lived in. From December to May, it would be bone dry. The bamboo bridges would be suspended high above. Piru would skip across the canal with her playmates to pick mangoes in the Mridhas' garden on the other side. In the monsoon, the canal would be overflowing. People would put up bamboo fences to trap fish. Boats would be ferrying people across all the time. Even at night Piru could hear the splash of the oars and the poles being used to steer the boats. Does the canal still exist? The one that soaked up all the water during droughts and overflowed its banks in the monsoon. A torrent of water would rush in unimpeded from the big river. Piru would lie in bed wondering how many fish had been trapped against the bamboo fence. All sorts of tiny fish. When the rains ended, Piru would bring home fish like shing, magur and koi, caught with nets cast from a boat submerged in the hyacinth-covered pond behind the Bhuiyans' house.

Slicing the fish with a big smile on her face, Piru's mother would say, "Get me some small icha tomorrow, Piru. You can catch them with a *gamchha*. I'll make you *bhorta*."

Piru would nod enthusiastically. All her father had to buy was the rice, oil and daal. Piru would wander around, collecting greens. When her father was out of work, her mother would find a job as a maid with well-off families. It was Piru who managed the household then. She would clean the house and gather the kindling. Piru used to have a goat. What was she called? Oh yes, Batashi. It was Piru who took her to graze in the fields. She would get jackfruit leaves from the Mridhas' garden to feed her goat. She would say, "When Batashi has kids, I'll give one to Ali, one to Halimon."

Halimon was Piru's soulmate. They would go bathing in the river together. Gather rice from the fields after the harvest. Collect greens. Catch small fry in their *gamchhas* in the canal. She had visited the Chaitra Sankranti fair with Halimon once. They had had so much fun. Taken rides on the Ferris wheel. Bought sweet *binni* and *batasha*. How anxious her mother had got because they had been late. She had all but burst into tears. That was how she was. She would rush to the fakir for charmed water and oil if Piru was even slightly ill. She would make strict vows. Her father would become desperate too. Where is she now? Where is he? Where is the village? Where, that huge blue river, those green fields, the free life by the canal?

A catastrophe came out of nowhere and swept everything away. Water from the big river flooded their village that monsoon, the murky currents submerging their homes. The water kept rising, covering the betel nut orchard and coming up all the way to where Piru and her parents lived. Their house was submerged. Perched high on a bamboo platform, they had watched as their home was destroyed. Living on the wheat provided as relief material, Piru and her family became destitute. By the time the omnivorous floods receded, the house had collapsed. Laments rose in the air everywhere in the village. The family sold Batashi and boarded a launch with the money from the sale as their only means. Everyone was saying they would find work in Dhaka. Like her father, Piru too thought there was plenty of money in the city. They would earn, save and go back home. Piru's father would build a house again.

But they never did go back. Her father operated a pushcart while her mother worked as a maid at three or four houses. By then their family had grown, with the arrival of a baby. Piru took care of her brothers in their slum dwelling in Malibagh, and did all the cooking. Sometimes she did the shopping as well. In her spare time she wondered how much longer it would take her father to save enough for them to go back home.

All kinds of people frequented the slum. One afternoon, her father was out with his pushcart, and her mother, at work. Ali was out with a sack, rummaging through the dustbins in the city to gather wood. Two strangers appeared. One of them said, "Your mother has had an accident. She's asked for you." Piru was dumbfounded at first. Then she left, sobbing, her little brother in her arms. The other man said, "Don't cry. Your mother's still alive. Come quickly. Pass the child to me."

Piru believed them. Even today, she doesn't understand why she had. She still doesn't know where the heartless thugs dumped her little brother.

One of them had dropped back with the child. The other one had made Piru get into a baby-taxi waiting on the road and taken her to a lane in old Dhaka. Piru didn't know her way around the city then. That was when she was taken into a completely different world. That man, along with two others, had made her body part of a ghastly game. Piru still trembles when she remembers that horrifying turn in her life. Then she was sold to Hiru, who had brought her here to Golapipatti.

Piru cries into her pillow. Has her father saved enough money by now to go back home? Imprisoned in the darkness that is her life, Piru knows nothing of what's happening. She has no idea whether her father is still looking everywhere for her. She doesn't know whether her mother still makes her favourite sweets and weeps, thinking of her.

Someone has just come up the stairs. It must be Jahanara, returning. She goes out on some nights. Comes back in a car. The next day, many of the women gather around her to listen in awe to stories of the whims of the rich.

Pushing Parul away, Piru eventually goes to sleep, her eyes still filled with tears.

FOUR

Shanti visits Yasmin in the afternoon. She's in her room. Marjina has got Thika Mashi to get them some meat from the market. Last night she got lucky and picked up several lucrative customers. Boiling rice on her oven, Huree comments sneeringly, "Look at her showing off on one night's earnings. Meat and fish for everyone. Won't last."

Stirring the meat on a pan with broken handles set on a kerosene stove, Marjina snaps at her, "Why are you so jealous, you bitch? I'll eat what I like with money earned from my own sweat."

Turning to Yasmin, she says, "What do you say, *buji*? Am I wrong? No one here can stand it when someone else does well. Always dying of jealousy."

Putting some kindling into her clay oven, Huree glares, "Who are you shouting at, you whore? Does anyone here live off anyone else? You pay rent, so do I. But I don't hide things like you do. We're whores, and people know us as whores. We're not like you, who covers her head and shakes her hips."

Huree's barb strikes home. There's some truth to what she has said. Marjina does go home to her village in Faridpur once every three or four months. Her family lives there. Her father is a cripple. Her brother works as a contract labourer in the rice mill near the village. He doesn't earn enough for them to live on. Marjina had come to the city with a woman from her village in search of work. Despite knocking on hundreds of doors, she hadn't got a job as a full-time maid anywhere. The one or two jobs she did get were part-time. Twenty taka as salary, along with a meal. How could Marjina survive on that? The rent for a slum room had risen. A room she could have got for five taka earlier wasn't available for less than thirty. Then there was her own food and clothing to take care of, besides sending money home to her starving family. Marjina had been forced to sell her body in the lanes. And then she had moved to this brothel. At seventeen, Marjina was voluptuous if not beautiful. She had got married in the village, but her husband didn't feed her. Now Marjina goes home at regular intervals. She takes saris for her mother, lungis for her father and clothes from the second-hand store for her brother and sister. She sends money home too. Everyone in the village is under the impression she works as a full-time maid for a family.

A furious Marjina is about to reply when Shanti comes up. Her fortunes have been constantly on the rise. She has taken an entire room on rent. Twirling the end of her new sari, Shanti says, "There you are, Yasmin Bu. I need a letter read out to me."

Shanti gets letters from home sometimes, addressed to Chheru's shop.

Now Marjina tells Huree stridently, "Check for yourself. There are plenty of others like me."

Flopping down on the cot, Shanti holds the postcard out to Yasmin. "It's a letter from home. Read it and write a reply for me."

Yasmin accepts the postcard. Shanti's backstory is almost identical to Marjina's. Shanti's elder brother has written that his daughter is getting married. He has requested some more money. Yasmin reads the letter out to Shanti. Shanti lapses into a sullen silence. Then she snarls, "It's always 'Send some money, send some money.' They have no idea how hard we work to earn it. Pay the rent. Bribe Mashi. Handle the police. It's not cheap, this bloody place."

Marjina says innocently, "Your poor brother is asking."

Shanti turns on Marjina for now. "Just what I expected you to say. Did his wife give me a bite to eat when I was starving? She locked herself in her room with her baby. I had no parents. Just the one brother, who didn't dare speak up for fear of his wife."

Shanti becomes quiet suddenly. Perhaps she recalls the desperate poverty-stricken days in the village. The man she was married to already had another wife. It was the other woman who controlled everything. Shanti's husband would often beat her black-and-blue after returning from the fields because of his first wife's complaints. One day, he had thrown her out. A helpless, heartbroken Shanti had returned home. Her sister-in-law had raged at her like a woman possessed, "Why are you here? I can barely feed my own family, how will I feed you too? Go find work and pay for your own meals."

Her brother had protested weakly, "Where will she go? Let her stay. She can eat leftovers."

His wife hadn't softened. "You think it's so easy? Where will she stay? We have just this one room. I can barely fit in here with the baby."

Shanti had pleaded plaintively with her. "I won't trouble you. I'll sleep on a sack in the room at the back. I'll eat whatever's left after your baby has eaten."

Shanti had moved in with her brother's family. But eventually she couldn't stay on. Her sister-in-law had made life hell for her, on top of which, she was starving. Shanti shifted to the whorehouse near the market.

Her sister-in-law had heaped abuse on her at the top of her voice. Her brother had begged her, "Don't make me an outcaste, Shanti."

Shanti had left the village, bitter, angry and hurt. When she thinks about it now, it surprises her that she sends money to this same brother. He has opened a stationery shop in the market town with that money. His fortunes have changed. A contemptuous smile flashes on Shanti's lips. Her brother no longer fears being an outcaste for writing to her for money. He tells everyone in the village proudly that his sister works as an ayah in a school.

Draining the starch from the rice, Huree says, "What's the matter, Shanti, did someone get your tongue?"

Shanti collects herself. Her voice rings out, "Write down, *buji*, I can't send so much money."

After a pause, she continues, "He says his daughter's wedding has been fixed, the groom is a good catch. Got some land of his own. I keep thinking, I've had no luck in my life, but let them have some."

Shanti jumps to her feet suddenly after a glance at the door. A man has appeared in the lane outside, just beyond their door. Many of the women don't accept customers at this hour, but then many do, too. The man comes up to the door. Marjina, Huree and the rest of them turn alert.

Their relaxed appearance of a few minutes ago is replaced by the flirtatious seductiveness of whores. Summoning an enticing smile to her lips, Marjina says, "In broad daylight, lover?"

Huree rolls with laughter. "Many gentlemen are afraid to visit us in the dark."

The man looks at them directly. "Who's Yasmin here?"

Looks are exchanged. Yasmin rises to her feet. Moyna is passing with a cup of tea she has bought for Jahanara. She stops on seeing the man and says loudly, "Why here, babu? Jahanara is on the first floor. Did you get confused?"

The man looks at her. "I'm not here for Jahanara."

Moyna pretends to be astonished. "Oh my! What are you saying? Weren't you here the other day? You got *bilati maal* to Jahanara's room."

Inspecting Moyna, the man says, "I'm here for Yasmin today."

Everyone is startled. Jahanara's customer at Yasmin's door! Is that even possible? No one dares to go anywhere near Jahanara's clients. And everyone knows that anyone who does visit Yasmin doesn't mention her, even by mistake, if he comes back. It's a mystery to all of them.

Only Mashi says, "She's educated, you see, so she can't make use of her body like other whores do. People come here for a change of taste, after all. Why will they like a woman who's so stiff?"

Moyna leaves. Yasmin goes up to the door. Looking askance at the tall man dressed in a *panjabi* and pyjama, she says, "I'm Yasmin. How did you know my name?"

The man looks at Yasmin too. He smiles faintly. "How difficult do you think it is to find out someone's name here?"

The lines on Yasmin's face harden. "I don't take clients in the daytime."

The man smiles again. "What if I tell you that I'm here to talk to you?"

Yasmin is astonished. The man is talking to her respectfully. What does he want!

Shanti leaves. Before going away, she says, "Bring your man in, *buji*. I'll come back later."

Marjina pours curry into the pot where the meat is cooking. Huree is done making the rice. Pushing the pan beneath the cot, she rises to her feet. Marjina says, "We're going out, let your man come in."

Marjina and Huree leave. They do not envy Yasmin. She doesn't get enough customers anyway. And besides, she works according to her whims. She cannot pay her rent. Doesn't get enough to eat. Still she goes three or four days at a stretch without taking a customer. The man waiting outside says, "Let's sit inside. We can't talk properly standing out here."

Yasmin retreats into her room. The man follows her in. He closes the door himself. Yasmin looks him in the eye. "I already said I don't take customers in the daytime."

The man lights a cigarette. "I'm told you're educated. You must have realised I'm not here as just another customer."

Yasmin doesn't respond. The man casts an eye around the damp, dirty room. Marjina's tin trunk lies in a corner. On it stands Huree's faded bag. Their grimy saris, blouses, petticoats, brassieres and towels hang from a line. Tins of spices, a kitchen blade, earthen basins and cans of oil are scattered everywhere. The fat and other discarded pieces from the meat are strewn on the floor. The floor is slippery with spilt water. The aroma of cooked meat emanates from Marjina's kerosene stove. A pile of tattered, oil-stained sheets and pillows is heaped on a corner of the bed. The man lifts his eyes. "This is the room you live in?"

Yasmin ignores the surprise in his voice. "Why, what's wrong with the room?"

"Just that it's . . . so tiny, so dank. Suffocating."

Yasmin laughs loudly. "And yet people like you visit such rooms to buy women's bodies."

The man looks at her, startled. After a pause, he says, "Such a hard life."

Yasmin curls her lips contemptuously. "Were you expecting to see a harmonium and tabla and liquor bottles and almirahs in a whore's room, like in a Saratchandra novel?"

Yasmin looks at him with glittering eyes. "I suppose you're looking for someone like Rajlakshmi or Chandramukhi. A heroine from a Bimal Mitra novel, perhaps? Actually . . ."

Yasmin stops. The man leans towards her, "Yes, what is it you want to say? Actually what?"

Wearily, Yasmin replies, "No, nothing."

"No, tell me. I want to hear."

Yasmin looks at the man piercingly. Then she slowly lowers her eyes to the ugly floor of her wretched room. "Actually, men can never think of such women as anything but butterflies. How attractive the character of Tarashankar Bandyopadhyay's Basanta was, wasn't she? But do you think she had no pain, no sorrows? Can you tell me why she . . . they . . . all of us here, are nothing but whores? We are human beings too. Just like your wives and daughters and sisters."

The cigarette has burnt down to the man's fingertips. He gazes with pained eyes at the agony on Yasmin's face.

Yasmin recovers. She summons a smile to her lips. "I won't send you back, since you've come all this way. But let me also tell you, my customers are never satisfied with me. Many of them abuse me. Many want their money back. Do you know why?"

Yasmin smiles an odd smile. "Every man has a beast within him. A beast with wild demands. People don't get from me the kind of vulgar gestures and dirty talk that they expect from women like us. I haven't been able to master those yet, you see."

Dumbfounded all this while, the man finally speaks. "How did you end up here? You're a misfit. You seem to be very well educated."

Yasmin looks stern. "I came the same way all other women do. Do any of you ever worry about how many women your collective blindness forces into this dark life every day?" Yasmin pauses before continuing, "Now, may I ask who you are and what your objective is?"

Throwing away the burnt-down cigarette, the man lights a fresh one. "I'm a writer. A journalist too. My name is Delwar Hussain."

Yasmin stirs the meat in Marjina's pot and lowers the flame. Then she turns back to the man. "So you're here in search of a plot for your novel. No one enters this lane without a motive. Very well, write a book about me. People will be repelled, but they'll still read it. Especially those who rail against obscenity in public and gobble down pornography in private. It'll sell very well. You'll make good money."

Delwar smiles faintly. "What if I tell you I want to hold up your misery to society?"

Yasmin bursts into laughter. "You're talking like the idealist hero of a novel. The kind of dialogue we hear from film stars on celluloid."

Delwar is shaken by her loud laughter.

By now, Yasmin has stopped laughing. She is gazing steadily at Delwar. Hatred radiates from her like a beam of light. Drawing random scratches on the bed with her fingernails, Yasmin says, "Who are the people in this society? Are those who visit whores to buy their own arousal not part of society? Are those who pay extra to take away beautiful prostitutes in their cars not part of society? Are those who extort money from us to get us our licences not part of society either? What happens when that money is converted to government earnings and served on every plate? What if I said that our money is the money that lets a minister ride in his official car to inaugurate a new factory?"

Delwar looks at Yasmin in utter consternation. "I heard of you and came here. The more I hear you talk, the more I'm surprised. I do not understand why you're living in this hell."

Yasmin turns away from his astonished gaze to take a moment before speaking. Then she says slowly, "Why are you asking me this? Ask the people in the world out there. Ask the mask-wearing, hypocritical society. The society that's rotting like the body of a leper with gaping wounds. I loathe it. I detest all gentlemen like you."

"But are you happy here?"

"Happy! Who's happy in a society in which people have no freedom, where everyone's bound by countless invisible chains? At least we don't hide behind a veil of pretence. The faces of the animals named men are not concealed behind masks."

Delwar lights another cigarette swiftly. "Must everything be accepted so meekly? Isn't it possible to protest?"

Yasmin looks up in surprise. "Who's going to protest?"

"Why not you and I? And many others like us. The women of this neighbourhood, for instance. Those who are victims of extreme injustice.

Once again, contempt flashes at the corners of Yasmin's lips. "Are you into politics? I know politicians deliver eloquent speeches. I was involved in politics too as a student. It makes me laugh now. I find the news of all the changes in your government hilarious. Can you tell me whether any of the governments that have run this country ever remembered the women in these brothels? Did they ever consider the way some people of this country, who were born as free citizens, are spending their lives like helpless, unthinking animals subjected to vicious torture? Their present is torment, their future is darkness. Who thinks about them?"

Yasmin is panting after her tirade.

Delwar is silent.

Marjina bangs on the door. "My curry must have burnt, *bu*. Are you done?"

Yasmin rises to her feet. "Will you leave now?"

Delwar gets up as well. "You seem so innocent, so pure."

Yasmin opens the door, "All humans are innocent. It's the environment that breeds sin. But then, you must be aware of the parameters of right and wrong in your society."

Delwar says, "I'll be back. I have to come to you."

Yasmin smiles mischievously. "As a man?"

"No, as a human being."

Delwar makes to leave. Marjina stands in the doorway, grinning slyly. "No one stays so long with Yasmin Bu. How much did you pay, lover?"

Delwar is startled. Taking a couple of notes out of his pocket, he holds them out hesitantly to Yasmin. "I hope you don't mind."

Yasmin gives him an odd smile. "Why should I mind? People come to us to pay."

She takes the money without hesitation. "Come again. It'll make me happy."

Delwar says as he is leaving, "I'll come to you as a friend."

Marjina, Huree and Shanti surround Yasmin after he's gone. Huree says, "That's a fat amount. What's going on, Yasmin Bu? Have you raised your rates overnight?"

Yasmin grins without replying. Handing Marjina a ten-taka note, she says, "Here you are. You'd lent it to me to pay the rent."

Bundling the note into the end of her sari, Marjina squats to take the meat off the stove. Yasmin tells Shanti, "What if this place closed down one day, Shanti?"

Shanti jumps in alarm. "What are you saying? What will happen to us? How will we survive? Heaven forbid! The things you say!"

Huree has bought a pitcher of water with Thika Mashi's help. Taking her blouse and petticoat off the line while she brushes her teeth with ground coal, she says, "Yasmin Bu, what's all this you're saying? Whorehouses never close down."

Yasmin smiles. "Why not? Of course they can."

Huree comments knowledgeably, "I get it. Must have come in the papers. But take my word for it, this business will never be closed down. Who will close it?"

Taking the meat off the stove, Marjina turns it off. "Don't tell us all this. We've seen these things. Everyone wants the flesh market to be open."

Huree says, "That one time, Badshah Ayub Khan passed a law that there would be no red light areas in the country. I used to live near the river bank then. The police came and surrounded the neighbourhood. Such destruction! And in the middle of all this, a group of policemen went into the girls' rooms. So much violence and bloodshed!"

Marjina arches her eyebrows. "And what came of it?"

Grinding her teeth and spitting out a black gob in front of the door, Huree says, "What could come of it? At the courts, they said they wouldn't file cases against us. The girls just scattered here and there. They were starving, so they chased customers wherever they could. I don't want any of that, we're so much better off here."

Yasmin looks at Huree. "Why, can't you and I and all of us live the way everyone else does, in regular homes with regular work?"

Shanti rolls with laughter. "Whores and homes. All those books you read have affected your brain, Yasmin Bu. Once you're branded, it never comes off."

Huree sneers. "To hell with living in a regular home. I'm fine as I am. I'll tell you the truth, the thought of spending the entire night with the same person makes me want to vomit. You get different pleasures from different men."

Marjina jokingly flicks at Huree's cheek with her fingertips. "Oh, my committed whorebitch! But then I agree, now that I've settled here I'll die here too. Let whatever happens happen in the world outside, what's it to us?"

Shanti says, "Who'll make room for us out there? The women there hate us even more than they hate lepers."

Yasmin is not to be put off. "Why do all of you think of yourselves as whores? Can't you think of yourselves as human beings instead?"

Shanti, Marjina and Huree laugh in unison. Shanti says, "We don't understand all these things you say, *bu*. But let me say this, you know Moti next door, she was so arrogant she tried to move out of this brothel. 'I'm not living in this hell anymore,' she said. 'I'd rather go back home and live on nothing but rice if I have to.' You think she was able do it? She came back less than two months later. The people in her village didn't leave her alone. What do you have to say to that?"

Yasmin has no answer to this. She searches for a response to these illiterate prostitutes' questions.

How is she to explain to them that they're living within the ulcer of society. They're keeping their bodies alive. But this cannot be called life.

Moving close to Yasmin, Shanti says, "Tell me something, is the government passing a law to abolish whorehouses?"

Yasmin shakes her head. "No, I haven't heard anything like that."

Huree goes up to the door to spit again. "Then we have nothing to worry about."

Yasmin looks at them for a while. They may be branded as wild, seductive and aggressive women, but at this moment, she cannot think of them as anything but ignorant, foolish children. Yasmin tells Marjina, "Give me a cigarette."

Yasmin doesn't smoke regularly like the other women here-abouts. Nor does she demand alcohol from her customers. Marjina takes out a cigarette with swift fingers and hands it to Yasmin.

FIVE

Mashi can be heard in the lane, "Where are all of you? Kazi Shaheb is here. Come on, quick, all of you. Pay your rent."

The sixty-year-old Kazi Shaheb is dressed in a long kurta and lungi. He sports a wispy white beard. Seated on a stool next to Mashi, he is speaking. Some of the women touch his feet to convey their respect. Kazi Shaheb lowers his eyes and summons a dazzling smile to bless them, "Live in peace and happiness."

Mashi has known Kazi Shaheb for a long time. Many backbiters among the old-timers say he used to be Mashi's regular customer in his youth. He has given up his worldly ways now. The last time he was here to collect rent, he had been chatting with Kanchan. "You see, Kanchan Miah, I am no longer interested in the pleasures of this world. I've spent three generations on earth. But the Hadis forbids me from denouncing the householder's life."

It's not just Kanchan but everyone else hereabouts who knows that Kazi Shaheb is performing his household duties quite well. Of course, the irreligious inhabitants of this brothel are not aware of his methods. Kazi Shaheb has a shop selling tyres and tubes and cycle parts in old Dhaka. He also owns a warehouse in Chawkbazar. And the earnings from rooms he gives on rent in whorehouses fetch him a decent amount too.

Mashi asks Kazi Shaheb with the familiarity of a member of the family, "How are the kids?"

Kazi Shaheb's face lights up with a smile. "They're all well. You do know I've married off my eldest daughter. The groom's a doctor. Earns quite well. The younger girl is going to college. BA exam this year. Her mother says not to hurry with her wedding. Says she'll pass her MA too and teach in a college."

Kazi Shaheb's smile widens. "My eldest son looks after the business. How much longer will I live? Here today, gone tomorrow. Let them take charge of what is theirs. I've had the younger son admitted to engineering college."

Mashi says, "Do your children know of this rental income?"

Kazi Shaheb frowns. "*Tauba, tauba*! What do you think you're saying, Sati? How can I tell them? They're modern educated children. What if they misunderstand? I would have wound down this business. If I don't it's only because these women are able to make a living, they can feed themselves. I charge low rents. Anyone else would have asked for twice as much."

Bokul is at the head of the queue with the money. Holding out a week's rent, she says, "The rainwater comes in through the ceiling, *chachajaan*. Makes things very difficult. Customers refuse to come in when the roof is dripping. If you could have it repaired. The rains are almost here."

There's a beatific smile on Kazi Shaheb's face. "What to do, my girl? You'll have to make do. The whole house will have to be demolished if the roof has to be repaired. Can I afford it all by myself? What do you people say?"

Shanti, Huree and Mamata are also standing there. Taking the notes from Bokul and counting them, Kazi Shaheb throws a glance at the others. "Well, girls? How are all of you?"

All of them are counting out their rents. Mamata is younger than the others. A little arrogant too. Kazi Shaheb turns to her. "I hear you're giving up your room?"

Mamata snarls in response, "Of course I will. Your ramshackle room isn't exactly cheap. Here's your money. There's ten taka less."

A wave of furrows appears on Kazi Shaheb's brow. "Less? Why should it be less? Aren't you taking in customers at night?"

Mamata answers blandly, "How will I pay you if I don't earn enough?"

Mashi jumps in. "I see you've learnt to talk back. What about all the new clothes and the movies? Why can't you pay your rent? Pay up, pay up now."

Mamata's shoulders stiffen. "I'll give it to Mashi next week."

Kazi Shaheb turns to Mashi in discontent. "I'm telling you, Sati, you must collect the rent for all the rooms. I've given you the responsibility, after all."

Mashi shouts back, "Are you saying I cheat you because you've given me the responsibility? I always collect the rent properly. When one or two don't pay, you turn up."

Kazi Shaheb smiles. "Now you're angry. Do you think I don't trust you? I've known you for so many years. Collecting the rent is just an excuse for me to visit. I get a chance to see how all of you are doing. Do you think my heart doesn't beat for these girls? Allah uses me to ensure they make a living."

Turning to Mamata, he says gently, "Give the money to Mashi, all right? Why don't you understand that you're able to make a living thanks to me? You have no idea about the world. How tough it is for people to survive. Where would all of you have been if I didn't give you these rooms at such low rents?"

Everyone hands over their rents and disappears. Some even tell themselves, *Kazi Shaheb is truly an angel. What a lovely thing he has said. It's true, where would we have been if he hadn't rented out his rooms to us. We would have had to beg, or die, on the street.* They cannot imagine what else might have happened. And Kazi Shaheb is not heartless like the owners of other brothels. He doesn't beat the women up to extract his dues.

Kazi Shaheb asks Mashi, "What news of your Phulmoti *bibi-jaan*? She's gone and had a child. I didn't give her the room for free."

Mashi says softly, "The girl's luck has deserted her. She's as shrivelled as a strand of rope. Who will come to her?"

Kazi Shaheb looks stern. "What's that got to do with me? Let her give up the room if she can't pay. Let her walk the streets with her child, begging for alms. I can't allow losses to be made from my rooms. Send for Phulmoti."

Someone fetches Phulmoti. She appears hesitantly, holding her child. Kazi Shaheb probably does not notice her famished, miserable appearance. He observes neither the dark circles under her eyes nor the ugly jutting out of her jawbones. Her unkempt, unclean hair, devoid of even a drop of oil, billows out around her face. She is wearing a dirty, faded sari and no blouse. Phulmoti stands diffidently, covering her head with the oil-stained end of her sari.

Kazi Shaheb roars, "*Kire, maagi*? When are you vacating the room? You haven't paid your rent for a month."

Phulmoti drags her big toe across the dust. "Give me a few more days, *chacha*. The baby's not well."

Kazi Shaheb mocks her. "The baby's not well. You didn't think of all this when making the baby? How can a whore have a baby?"

Phulmoti murmurs, "What can I do? Can't throw her away."

Kazi Shaheb grows even more furious. "Has Mannan's shop run out of pills? Can't you buy pills? Don't tell me all this. Pay the rent or get out."

Phulmoti suddenly flings herself at Kazi Shaheb's feet, sobbing, "*Chachajaan*! You're like my father. We depend on you. Are you going to throw me out?"

Mashi shouts at her, "Shut up, *maagi*! No need to put up this show of crying. Hasn't anyone ever worked with a baby here?"

Phulmoti continues weeping. "What can I do? The baby just won't get well. I don't get enough to eat. I can't feed her. Can't give her a drop of medicine. Take her with you, *chacha*, give her away to someone."

Kazi Shaheb curls his lips. "You expect me to soil my hands with your bastard child! Listen, *maagi*! I want my full rent next week. Or else I'll send Hiru. He'll stick a knife into your belly and your baby's and pull out my dues. You think I don't know how to get money out of a whore like you?"

Phulmoti lifts her eyes. Her tears fall on her baby. Kazi Shaheb screams at her, "Get out of my sight!"

Phulmoti goes away. Once she is out of their view, she gnashes her teeth. "Treacherous old swine. May the evil eye fall on your family. May Allah make all your descendants die."

Kazi Shaheb rises to his feet. "I'll go now, Sati. I'll drop by my daughter's house on my way back. She isn't well."

Mashi asks, "What's happened to the girl?"

Kazi Shaheb looks pleased. An indulgent smile spreads across his face. "I'm going to have a grandchild. The girl can't eat anything. I'm going to buy her some *doi* with this money."

Mashi sounds elated. "It's good news, then. You'll see your grandchild soon. You must buy me an expensive sari when you do, I'm telling you right now."

"Of course I will. Pray that all goes well with her."

Kazi Shaheb leaves with a smile and laden pockets.

Climbing up the stairs, Mamata hears Phulmoti furiously dashing her baby to the floor and screaming, "Die! Die! Die now, you bitch! Why did Allah send you to me?"

The baby cries out at the top of her voice. At once, Phulmoti's rage is drowned in tears. "What for? What did you come to a whore's womb for? What will I do with you now?"

No one has time for Phulmoti's lament. Not even Mamata. She races up the stairs to Jahanara's door.

The door is open. Jahanara is in bed, lying on her stomach, her clothes draped loosely around her. Moyna is massaging her back. Running her eye across Jahanara's glossy, gleaming room,

Mamata looks at the nude on the wall. Moyna turns towards her. "What is it, Mamata, what do you want?"

Mamata is on her guard. "I came to meet Janu Bu, *khala*."

Jahanara lifts her eyes. They're bloodshot. She had had that horrible headache last night. Not even three Sonaril tablets had succeeded in taming her wild, uncontrollable headache and soothing her nerves. Thrashing about in pain, Jahanara had ripped up the pillow and mattress. Shattered bottles and crockery. Smashed her head against the wall. After flailing all night, she had finally gone to sleep at dawn, waking up much later.

Lifting her head with much effort, Jahanara says, "What is it, *bibi*, what do you want?"

Mamata is pleased at being addressed as *bibi*. She realises that despite her physical pain Jahanara is in a good mood. When she is, she teases Mamata by calling her Bobita or Kobori or Shabana. Mamata is the butt of this particular joke with many of the women here. There's a reason for it. Mamata is addicted to films. She starves if necessary to watch movies. She copies the ways of film stars. She orders her tailor to replicate the clothes of actresses. Of course, she earns quite handsomely now. Mamata takes in eleven or twelve customers every night. She gets tips too. Many people in this brothel know that Mamata from Barisal ran away from home to become a film star. But leave alone a star, she has never even appeared on screen. After bouncing around places good and bad, and whirling around in the black eddies of this city, she has been pitched headlong into life in this murky lane. She still dreams of the movies. She uses her tips to buy film magazines. Tries to practise the styles and fashions of the stars. To her, every customer seems to have descended from the world of film stars. The dream is shattered almost every day. None of the men who come here to fulfil their bestial desires betrays any sign of being a hero. They all seem to be villains. And still Mamata, lying on her filthy bed in her dilapidated room in a haze of Sonaril tablets and cheap liquor, loses herself in the technicolour world that she conjures up. This hideous, ramshackle building, the dirty lane, the stinking drains, the grotesque quarrels, the violent fights, the obscene jokes, all recede into the distance. Mamata forgets the dark side of the world of cinema, which has led her to this life.

Her eyes half-open, Jahanara says to Mamata, "That's a sexy dress."

Mamata smiles. She is wearing trousers and a red shirt, with a pattern of lace instead of fabric covering her breasts. Mamata has padded her bra with sponges to make the curves of her body sharper and more prominent. She doesn't tell Jahanara how long she has had to save the money to get this outfit made, an outfit she has seen on a movie heroine. Standing there for a few moments, she says, "Will you lend me your scissors, Janu Bu? I'll return them quickly."

Moyna lifts her eyes. "What do you want scissors for?"

Mamata keeps her smile vibrant. "To cut my hair."

Moyna rolls her eyes. "Cut your hair? What for? Are you giving up worldly life?"

Clutching her long tresses, Mamata laughs. "You don't keep track of the world, *khala*. Do you think I'm going to get a crew cut? These days, movie stars cut their hair differently in front. It looks like short hair, but they still have long hair at the back."

Still massaging Jahanara's back, Moyna sneers. "Now a Golapipatti woman wants to be a lady. The things you see if you live long enough!"

Jahanara stops Moyna. "Be quiet! What do you know of all this? The days of whores like you are past. I go out, I know these things."

Looking at Mamata, she says, "Come in, Mamata. The scissors are on the shelf there. Take them, but don't forget to bring them back. If you don't return them, I swear I'll have your head shaved."

Jahanara begins to laugh. Mamata enters without hesitation, picks up the scissors, and leaves.

Parul is washing her clothes. Mamata calls her, "*Ei*, Paruli, come quick! I've brought the scissors."

Wringing her sari, Parul says, "Wait a minute. I'll just put this on the line to dry and be back."

Sitting in the room, Mamata opens a film magazine to examine a well-known heroine's hairstyle. Parul returns in a few minutes. The younger women defer to Mamata as much as they envy her. She has a heart of gold. She gives cosmetics to Parul sometimes.

Mamata has already cut some of the hair in front with the help of the mirror. She hands Parul the scissors. "Cut the hair at the back in steps on both sides."

Mamata takes a packet of cigarettes and a matchbox out of her hip-pocket. "Want one?"

Concentrating on cutting Mamata's hair the way it's shown in the photograph, Parul shakes her head. "Not now. Will you treat me to a cup of tea for cutting your hair?"

Mamata enjoys a great deal of freedom now. Just like Piru and Parul, she too was one of Hiru's purchases. She has money to spare now that she is in business independently. She pays her rent. Gets clothes made. Smokes or drinks a cup of tea whenever she wants. The way her income is shooting up, she may soon become a woman of consequence around here.

Sometimes Mamata tells Piru and Parul and Kusum stories while having a smoke. "I had a customer yesterday, I can't tell you, looks exactly like Razzak. A sweet-talker too. A little scared. College student."

Piru isn't enthusiastic. Parul listens in rapt attention.

She envies Mamata at these moments. Mamata moves around the neighbourhood with the rhythm of a dancer. She leans over the crumbling bannister and sings film songs.

Running the scissors through Mamata's hair, Parul says, "Do you know that a man spent a lot of time in Yasmin Bu's room the other day?"

Mamata shoots back, "Is she even a woman? Who would visit her?"

Parul laughs in agreement, "Those airs she puts on, like she's a queen. I heard she holds meetings with others."

"Hmm, she does read the paper every day."

"You're from a decent family too, Mamata. But you don't stay aloof from us."

"Me and that *maagi*? She's more like a man than a woman. How can you compare us, Paruli! She's too complicated for me. Just you wait, I'm definitely getting into the movies one day. I've

heard the heroines used to come from our kind of neighbour-
hoods in the past."

Parul puts the scissors down. "Give me a drag. You smoke
too much these days."

Mamata chuckles as she hands her cigarette to Parul. "It's not
new, I used to smoke from the time I lived at home. My parents
didn't know. A boy taught me. A college student who used to live
next door. He'd stare at me through the window. I smiled at him
one day. That was it. after that, he started sending me reams of
letters."

Parul asks inquisitively, "Did he love you? Did you love
him?"

Mamata smiles knowingly. "You think it was just one boy
who loved me? And do you suppose I didn't love many boys too?
I'd watch a film and fall in love every day. I fell in love with anyone who looked like a movie star. The last one got me to leave
home by promising to make me an actress."

Parul bursts with an unfamiliar envy. They live in the same
brothel. But there are no such thrilling incidents in Parul's life.
Hiru bought her and set her up here. She's fed up of the abuse
she has to face because he hasn't yet made a profit on his invest-
ment. She doesn't even get two square meals a day. How much
further will Mamata race ahead? Already she is so much in
demand. And such a colourful past. She has accepted the love
and attention of so many men already. Parul feels angry. And the
rage arising from her own impotence makes Mamata its target.
Parul doesn't yet know what love is. She is aware of no variations
on the mechanical physical exchange between men and women.
It seems to her that Mamata has selfishly snatched away Parul's

right to know these things and is enjoying them alone. Mamata has blossomed into a butterfly despite the misery and cruelty and suffering in this brothel. At this moment, Parul has forgotten her friendship with Mamata. The scissors in her hand seem to demand revenge for her own inability. Mamata frees her head with a jerk. By then, most of her hair has found its way into Parul's hand. A furious Mamata jumps up, "What did you do, you bitch, you pig?"

Overcoming her silence, Parul stammers, "I don't know how it happened. I didn't realise."

A wary Parul does not reveal that she has clipped Mamata's beautiful cloud-like hair out of jealous rage. Gathering her shorn hair, Mamata throws a glance at Parul's secretive eyes. Then grabbing the scissors from her, she pounces on Parul. Kusum, Piru and many others come running at their fighting, screaming and abuses. Piru is the first to shriek in terror, "Murder! She's being murdered!"

The sharp blades of the scissors are plunged into Parul's cheek. Blood is gushing out. Both their clothes are blood-soaked. Jahanara comes up the stairs, Kanchan and Moyna behind her. Many others are crowding round. Kanchan kicks the combatants apart. "The cunts are going to kill each other without anyone's help."

Jahanara snatches the scissors from Mamata. "Is this what you borrowed my scissors for, you bitch?"

Mamata tosses her raggedly cut short hair. "I'm going to kill the *khanki* today. She cut my hair off out of jealousy."

She charges at Parul again. Kanchan delivers a mighty slap on her face. "Fuck off. Don't show us your temper. The police will take you away."

Parul has been severely injured. The bleeding won't stop. Moyna says, "Just see what she's done. It would have been all over if the scissors had landed in her neck instead of her face."

Kusum holds a torn rag to Parul's cheek. She tears a strip of cloth to bandage it. Still, the blood keeps soaking through. Parul is weeping. She did it on an impulse. She didn't know Mamata would turn violent.

Hiru arrives, having heard the news. Everyone makes way for him. He begins to slap and kick both of them straightaway. Returning to her room, Jahanara says, "What's the use of beating them up now? Get her cheek stitched by a doctor or the girl will bleed to death."

Hiru roars, "Let her die. Let her. I'll throw the body away."

The fracas continues. Mamata goes up to the roof after some time, wiping her eyes. No one takes Parul to the doctor. She gets some ointment from Mannan's shop, smears it on her cheek, and lies down. People forget the whole thing soon. Phulmoti had come with her baby in her arms. On her way back, she stops at Jahanara's door on a whim. Peeping in, she says, "I have something to tell you, Jahanara Bu."

An annoyed Jahanara sits up in her bed. "Can't even lie down in peace for a bit *shala*. One bitch has already committed murder with my scissors. What do you want, *maagi*?"

Phulmoti shrinks in hesitation and fear. Wanly she says, "Will you lend me twenty taka?"

Jahanara looks her up and down with widened eyes. "Twe . . . e . . . nty?"

"Yes, I'm in trouble."

Phulmoti lifts her eyes from the floor and pours her heart into her plea.

Jahanara is stern. "It's not as though I don't lend money, I do. But how can I trust you to return it? I heard Kazi has asked you to vacate the room."

Phulmoti crumbles in humility. "Please, *bu*, please! Allah will increase your earnings. My baby will starve to death otherwise. I haven't eaten in days. No milk in my breasts. The baby's dying of hunger."

Jahanara looks at the baby in her arms in silence. Then she gets out of bed and hands two ten-taka notes to Phulmoti. "Here you are. Get milk for the baby. Don't forget to return the money."

Phulmoti melts in gratitude. "I will, *buji*, I will. I'll return your money as soon as I get a few customers."

Jahanara shuts the door. Her head is aching again. She loses all balance when this headache starts. Her lush body, luxurious room, monetary affluence all become irrelevant. She detests everything. She starts hating her regular, revered customers, who indulge her in every way. The headache has become more frequent of late. Something has happened to Jahanara ever since that wretched man told her all those strange things. She can still remember the message in his eyes. She feels the eyes had tried to say, "Beautiful Jahanara! You're nobody's wife or mother or sister. You will only exist as long as your body is attractive. Then you will lie crippled like that hag Golapjaan by the drain one day. Or you will rush around maddened by disease like Rohimon."

Jahanara shakes these thoughts off and scolds herself. She hasn't risen to the top in this business overnight. She has suffered many ordeals. Why is she giving so much importance to the ghostly presence of that man? Her admirers are not ordinary people. They wield power and influence amongst others. And besides, Jahanara owns two liquor shops in the neighbourhood. At the very least, she can spend her old age in comfort as a landlady with a big income. Still, she is beset by a doubt, a fear, sometimes. Jahanara remembers a formidable whore named Manjari who used to live in her previous neighbourhood. Manjari had a reputation as an adept prostitute. Everyone was in awe of her. She would get frequent calls to people's houses. Rich clients. She used to own liquor shops. Made a lot of money too. But Manjari's hired goon killed her one day. He became the owner of all her property. What if Jahanara's fate holds something similar for her? There's no such thing as trust in the brothel. She even has suspicions sometimes about the trustworthy Kanchan. She knows he has his eye on her liquor shop. She doesn't have a licence for the shop. And that's the trouble. Should she get rid of him with the help of other thugs? But how will that solve the problem? Ten more Kanchans will spring up. Each of them even more untrustworthy than the original.

Jahanara feels disturbed. She seeks a sanctuary whenever such thoughts come to her head. She wants to cling to something. What comfort will she seek? Should she ask those powerful womanisers for help? But they have their reputations, their homes, their families. Will any of them hold out a hand in support? An uneasy Jahanara opens her door and steps outside. She says loudly, "O Moyna, get me a bottle from the shop."

Moyna comes a little later with the bottle. She says, "You had a tough night, you should be bathing and eating now. Why the bottle?"

Uncorking the bottle and pouring the contents into a glass, Jahanara says, "Shut up and sit down, you bitch. I'll do as I please."

Moyna sits by the door with an unhappy expression. Jahanara drains her glass and refills it. She says, "Don't you want some?"

Moyna knows the question means she has to have a drink too. She's pleased. She cannot afford foreign liquor. It's only thanks to Jahanara that she gets a sip now and then. She fetches a glass. Jahanara fills it herself. As she drinks, Moyna observes the colour of Jahanara's eyes changing. She knows Jahanara is not a big drinker. The alcohol hits her quickly.

Jahanara says, "Moyna!"

Moyna is also feeling good after a few sips. Lightly, she replies, "Tell me, *bu*."

Jahanara scolds her, "*Shala maagi*, why do you call me *bu*? Don't you know my name is whore?"

Moyna does not reply.

Jahanara screams at her again, "Cat got your tongue? Where did that swine go, that son of a bitch who paid me fifty without even lying down on my bed?"

Setting her glass down, Moyna says, "The bastard comes quite often. Spends hours in Yasmin's room every time."

Jahanara flares up. With bloodshot eyes, she says, "Yasmin's room? Why, did the son of a bitch get scared after seeing Jahanara? You know Moyna, he's an effeminate impotent swine. Let me know if he comes back. I'll make sure he sleeps in the lane for ever."

Moyna realises that Jahanara is drunk. She doesn't reply. Putting away the half-finished bottle, Jahanara suddenly puts her arms around Moyna and begins to sob uncontrollably. "Moyna *re*. Someone will kill me one day. I'll be murdered. Will you protect me, Moyna? Tell me you will."

Moyna guides a tottering Jahanara to the bed. She runs her hands over Jahanara's brow. Jahanara clings to her hands, slurring, "Moyna *re*, don't abandon me, Moyna. Tell me, Moyna, what will happen to me? What?"

Moyna feels a stab of fear. She does not know the answer. Possibly no one in the brothel does. No one knows what lies in each of their uncertain futures. Jahanara's drunken rambling questions bounce off the silent walls of the decrepit building.

SIX

It's been raining incessantly for the past few days. Sometimes hard, sometimes gently. The entire lane is awash in mud and water. The filth in the drains is rising to the surface. The dirty rainwater has entered some of the rooms.

The rain intensifies just before evening. Thunder reverberates in the sky. Lightning flashes constantly. Shanti has moved into Zarina's room. She cannot remain in hers in the rain. Raising her sari to her knees, Shanti is piling all the things in the room on the cot. Here too the water is swirling ankle-high. Covering the grimy, tattered blankets and pillows with a torn, dirty plastic sheet, Zarina shouts, "Where are you, Kusmi? Get a mop and sweep the water out."

Hurling filthy abuse at the rain, Shanti says, "Kusum went to the shop." Water is pouring from the roof. Placing a battered pan and bucket beneath the stream, Shanti says, "It's impossible to be in my room, Zari. I'll have to stay here today. How to take in customers today in the rain, though?"

Shanti's sari is wet below her waist. Zarina is soaked too. Looking at the pile of plates, pots, stoves, tins of spices and other things, she says "Will anyone come in this rain?"

Kusum appears, soaked to the skin. Pulling a packet out of the end of her sari, she hands it to Shanti, saying, "Here's your *muri*. It got wet in the rain."

Shanti discovers that it has turned soggy. She snarls at Kusum, "Why didn't you borrow Mashi's umbrella? The whole thing's wasted."

Kusum is wet and bedraggled. Her hair is dripping. Her lips are black. Wringing the water out of her sari, she says, "Mashi never parts with her umbrella. What can I do?"

Zarina sneers. "As if we'll eat up the miserly hag's umbrella." Kusum is feeling cold. Hesitantly she asks, "Will you give me a dry sari to wear, Shanti Buji? I'm very cold."

Shanti gives her an earful before turning away. "Go take a look at my room, woman. It's flooded. Everything I have is sopping wet. How will I find a dry sari for you?"

Zarina softens at Kusum's frozen appearance. "You're shivering like a little bird. I have an old sari in the trunk, let me get it for you. Can you get the mop and sweep the water out?"

Kusum grows cheerful at the promise of a dry sari. She begins to sweep the water out with great enthusiasm.

Rummaging in the basket for a couple of onion slices, Shanti garnishes the *muri*. She hasn't cooked this afternoon because of the rain. She's in a foul mood. She'll have to pay for the nights she spends in this room. So much trouble when it rains. She was wrong to take the room she had originally.

Shanti calls out to the others. "Zarina, Kusum, come have some *muri*."

Zarina hasn't been able to cook either. Her clay oven is full of water. Almost everyone in the neighbourhood is in the same situation. Everyone's roof is dripping. Most of the rooms are flooded with the rainwater overflowing from the drains. It's impossible to light stoves and cook. Some of them get food from a restaurant on such days. Others have to content themselves with tea and *muri*. Many starve. Getting the water out of the room with great effort, Kusum uses planks and bricks to block the inlet and rises to her feet. She is shivering, wet and cold. Zarina tosses an old tattered sari at her. "Wipe your head and change into this."

Kusum strips in front of them, dries her body and wraps the sari around herself.

Transferring a fistful of *muri* into her mouth, Zarina says, "The girl has no flesh on her. How will she? She has to eat first."

Using her feet to wipe the slush on the floor, Kusum sits next to Shanti, who gives her some *muri*. Kusum is gratified. Shanti and Zarina have paid for the *muri*. Kusum isn't entitled to a share. Eating, she says, "That hag Golapjaan will die today."

Zarina curls her lips. "You think she'll die so easily. She has nowhere to live. Her legs are crippled. She can barely crawl about. No food. Still the hag is alive."

Kusum says, "No, *bu*, she's lying by Mannan's shop, getting soaked in the rain. She won't survive this time."

Shanti looks pensive. "Think about it, Golapjaan was also like us once. She's old now. Blind. Can't walk. She'll be found dead by the drain one day. The *dom* will throw her body away."

They are silent at this. All three of them are lost in thought. The shadow of their own inevitable fate makes them pensive in the darkness wrought by the rain. Kusum is heartbroken. She has just seen the seventy-year-old Golapjaan curled into a ball, soaking in the rain, only half-protected by the roof of Mannan's shop. Someone walking past with an umbrella kicked her aside, accompanied by foul language: "This bitch has all the lives of a cat, she just doesn't die."

Kusum had seen the raindrops fall into the hag's open mouth. With a trembling hand, the old woman had tried to shield her face now and then from the sharp arrowheads of the rain.

Rubbing her muddy feet together, Kusum says, "Can't we let the hag sleep in our room this one night, Zari Bu?"

Zarina sneers. "What a princess of generosity. What's that saying again? No place to save your own life, a dozen maids to serve your wife. Is the room our inherited property which we can allow anyone to use free of cost?"

Finishing her *muri*, Shanti says, "Enough of the nonsense. Kusmi, push everything on the bed to the corner. Have to make some room for the lovers."

Kusum gets up. Doing as Shanti asks her to, she says, "Do you think anyone will come today? Not even dogs go out in so much rain."

Evening has arrived behind the fringed curtain of the rain. The wavering sound of the azan can be heard over the clatter of the raindrops.

Lighting a bunch of incense sticks, Zarina begins to dress up as usual. She's in a foul mood. The rain not only makes life difficult, it also cuts into business. There are far fewer customers. A few do turn up nevertheless. And many regular customers defy the weather to ensure attendance with their favourite whore.

The lights come on in every room despite the torrential rain. The fragrance of incense rises above the stench of dirty water. Chheru opens his liquor shop. A couple of customers gather there. To excite the men who have drunk too much this rainy evening, Nabu the eunuch sways in his costume, singing hoarsely:

The new tree is blooming
Don't break the branch
Or pluck the flower

Monsoon insects buzz around the pool of light cast by Chheru's shop. One by one, people enter the wet, slippery lane, choose their women for the night, do their bargaining, and go into the rooms. Shanti gets a customer despite the rain. Zarina and Kusum have to wait outside. Zarina smokes standing in the rain, keeping a sharp eye on the head of the lane for new customers. Kusum isn't feeling well. She has a pain in her back and chest. Her head is throbbing too. She coughs several times. Zarina barks at her in a bad temper, "Why are you coughing so much?"

Kusum answers, exhausted, "I don't feel well, will you check if I have a fever, *buji*?"

Zarina feels Kusum's forehead and chest with her palm. "You're right. You're burning up. Better not take in anyone tonight."

Kusum says dejectedly, "How will I get one in this weather anyway?" The rain comes down harder. The splashing and dripping of the water all around makes Kusum think she too is drowning in the rain, like Golapjaan. She craves a dry room and a dry bed. Darkness descends like a fine powder in front of her eyes. Kusum stands there, getting soaked in the rain, chilled to the bone.

Piru is in bed, dreaming of trapping shrimp in her *gamchha* in the village canal, along with Halimon.

Parul is flying with the wings of a fairy in her own dream. Like Jahanara, she is on her way to a high-paying tryst in a luxury car.

Next to her, Mamata is being swept along on a happy dream of her own. Her face appears on the enormous silver screen in a movie hall. Mamata is singing a love song. The audience is enchanted.

Suddenly an explosive sound rocks the house like an earthquake. Jahanara shoots upright in bed, her eyes laden with sleep. Shanti, Bokul, Marjina, Kusum, Zarina, Yasmin, Moti . . . all of them wake up. It's pouring outside. They cannot see one another in the impenetrable darkness. Someone's door is banging in the wind. There is a clattering sound on the tin roof. Zarina's first sensation on waking up is one of fear. Of dread. She remembers the tidal wave from the sea that arrived with a terrifying roar on just such a night, along with a tornado. Zarina of Khepupara had lost everything she had then, in 1970. Pimps had lured the penniless, bewildered Zarina to this city with promises of relief supplies.

Moti recollects the Hindu-Muslim riots all those years ago. She remembers that wretched night when the hoodlums had pounded on their door after setting fire to the house. The door had collapsed with just such a violent shaking. Moti had watched her parents, grandmother and two younger brothers being stabbed to death. After being raped, Moti had had to end up here, following the dictates of fate.

Bokul remembers being abducted by pro-Pakistan criminals from Mohammadpur during the Liberation War of 1971. Her heart had trembled with fear the same way that day.

Putting her arms around Zarina, Kusum trembles uncontrollably amidst the shouts and loud voices floating about in the darkness. A dreadful night seems to emerge like a giant spider from her subconscious. Driven mad by starvation because of the famine, she had left the village for the city along with her parents. They had had to beg on the streets. A decrepit ruin in the old city was their shelter for the night. Many victims of famine from the villages had gathered there for sanctuary. After filling their bellies with the food they had begged or scavenged for, when the different families had fallen asleep like dogs coiled up together, two trucks had come to a halt on the main road. The night had trembled with cries, shrieks and screams. The well-lit, elegant skyscrapers in the city had not woken up because of them. Nor had the policemen on duty at the police-station. The armed hooligans had taken away the homeless, starving girls and the young women who had come of age. One of them had clamped his hand on Kusum's mouth. "Don't you dare scream. We'll murder your entire family."

Kusum still doesn't know why so many anguished screams hadn't left even a scratch on the heart of the city. She doesn't know which criminals had hired the armed goons to snatch them from their parents' arms. Kusum trembles, holding Zarina.

In her darkened room, Yasmin feels a tremor wrack her body like an epileptic patient's. Where had the sound come from? Is the world being shaken to its foundations again? The shadow of another forest, full of wolves, dances in the darkness beneath Yasmin's eyelids. Yasmin was clutching her mother in a dark room, trembling constantly. A military convoy had surrounded their entire neighbourhood. Her father was saying, "Where's the boy, where's Kamal?"

Her mother had whispered, "He jumped over the kitchen wall at the back long ago."

Several pairs of boots were thudding against the door. A number of voices were bellowing, "Open the door, you swine."

Her father had taken a few steps forward. "Let me open the door." Her mother had shouted in a stricken voice, "No, don't!"

Her father had said, "They will break it open otherwise. Kamal must have got away to a safe distance by now."

He had opened the door. And a violent, apocalyptic storm had burst in on them.

Her father had collapsed face first when a bayonet was thrust into his belly right at the door. No one in the family had been spared punishment for the offence of giving shelter to a freedom fighter. Yasmin had been dragged across the blood-soaked corpses of her parents and siblings and forced into a jeep along with their servant Ali. Yasmin had found out in the jeep that it was Ali who had informed the marauding armed forces about Kamal.

Yasmin had had to appear in front of the Major after inhuman physical torture. She had been forced to make a statement about Kamal. Kamal was her brother's friend. Her brother had died in the university hall on the night of 25 March. The family had known that Kamal had joined the Liberation Army. In Dhaka on an operation, he had taken shelter in their house, stashing weapons and ammunition with them. He had taken them away later. Yasmin had no idea where he had come from, where he had gone, or who his companions were. The Major had not believed her. They had continued punishing her by different means. Eventually Yasmin had been packed off with many other abducted women. She had spent six interminable months in a harem, fulfilling the lusts of the human beasts in soldiers' uniforms who were arrogant enough to fight a war against unarmed people. Then the sun had risen. The winter had receded to make way for the breeze of freedom and cries of triumph. Yasmin had been freed. She had all but lost her mental equilibrium. By the time Yasmin could look at the world through healthy eyes, she was in a shelter for assaulted women. The warrior sons returned to their mothers. The wheel of human life began to turn at its natural pace once again. A number of heartrending reports were published about them in the newspapers without revealing their names. Reading them with great interest, people breathed a sigh of relief, telling themselves, "I'm so lucky it didn't happen to my wife or daughter or sister."

Then the government ceremoniously elevated each of them to the pedestal of 'Birangona.' Young men were encouraged to marry the Birangonas and lead them back to regular life. People read in the newspapers that many liberal young men stepped up to accept the assaulted women as their life partners. It was just Yasmin's luck. She had been forced to witness her family being killed. But despite her long stay at the shelter, no other relatives had showed up. One day, she took some money from the super-intendent and went on a rickshaw ride. She discovered that even if Dhaka had forgotten her, she had not forgotten its roads and alleys. She knew her Chacha's address. She asked the rickshaw to wait when she went in—who knew whether her uncle and his family were alive or not.

Chacha was reading the newspaper. He jumped as though he'd seen a ghost. "Is it really you? You're alive?"

Yasmin discovered that her uncle's home and household effects were intact.

He stammered in dismay, "They'd taken you to the canton-ment. I made enquiries everywhere."

By then her aunt and cousins had gathered at the door. They were staring at her as though she was not of this earth, but an alien who had found her way here.

Chacha said, "Where have you come from?"

Yasmin realised that the tide had turned against her. Coldly, she said, "From the shelter. There are many other girls like me there."

Chacha suddenly appeared animated. "So you're here. I'm glad. Have some tea with us."

Yasmin levelled a long look at him. "Were all of you all right?"

"Yes. No. We managed. Your Chachi left for the village with Rina and Tina the very next day after the army raided your house."

Yasmin asked, "Did you know they had taken me away?"

"How could I not? Everyone in the family had come to know. How panicked we all were. Everyone had wives and daughters, after all." "Why didn't you look for me after independence?"

"Look where? I didn't think you'd have survived."

"You'd probably have been happier if I'd died. Look, Chacha, not everyone dies. Some are forced to live on with their memories of the torment."

Chacha went up to her. "Sit down. Calm yourself."

Yasmin turned. "I won't sit. How's everyone else?"

Chacha began to reel off a list of who had lived, who had died, and whose property had been destroyed.

The rickshaw-driver was ringing his bell. Yasmin said, "I'll go now." Her uncle glanced at his wife. "So soon? Have a cup of tea with us." After a pause, he added inconsequentially, "If only your father hadn't let that fellow into the house."

Yasmin wheeled back to face him. "Was it a very big crime? It was because boys like them fought and girls like me were raped that people like you can breathe freely in an independent country."

Yasmin walked out. Chacha followed her. "You have no reason to be angry, Yasmin. I have grown-up daughters at home, after all. I have to get Rina and Tina married. Why're you blaming me alone? After 16 December, even your mother's brothers said, we want Yasmin to be dead. Let her not have to come back."

"Was it shame they feared? Or was it the lack of courage to accept the truth?"

Chacha looked chastened. "You passed the MA Preliminaries, didn't you? The government is offering jobs to Birangonas. I can try for you if you like. Just don't tell them I'm your uncle."

"Chacha!" Yasmin almost screamed in anguish. Then she continued, "Am I not your brother's daughter? Am I not a woman of this country? Am I a Birangona even to you?"

"It's not a disrespectful name."

"I don't think it is. But you and many others probably do."
"What are you saying? Everyone sympathises with you." "Pities us, you mean."

"You've changed, Yasmin."

"Your dearest Rina and Tina would have also changed, just like me, if they had had to spend agonising days and months in the same misery and suffering."

Yasmin returned to the shelter. She didn't visit anyone else on the basis of a family relationship or old acquaintanceship. She had already seen the reflection of all her relatives' and friends' hearts in her uncle. Chacha wasn't completely inhuman, however. He visited her a few times. He told her, "I've arranged for a good job for you, Yasmin. Someone's taken possession of your house, however. Take the job. I'll ensure your house comes back to you."

Yasmin did not reply at first. Then she said, "You're the one who told me the house has been looted. That not even a thread has been left behind. I don't even have my certificates. How will I go for the interview?"

Her uncle was well-connected. He pulled enough strings to get Yasmin as far as the interview board. But she withdrew, recoiling as though she had been struck by lightning. She had only one identity to use as her asset everywhere. The officials on the interview board were clearly curious. Yasmin could read their faces. "You are a Birangona. The marauding soldiers raped you." One of the members of one board asked her, "You're a Birangona. Where did they capture you? How did it happen?"

Yasmin answered all the questions accurately. Another one asked, "What sort of torture did they inflict on you?"

Yasmin pushed her chair back and stood up. "The kind of torture cruel, heartless men inflict on women."

After a pause, she said sharply, "The same way that all of you are satiating your curiosity by probing the gaping wound in my heart for your enjoyment."

One of the elderly officials said, "Sit down, *Ma*, sit down. We understand, you are upset."

Yasmin burst out, "It's all of you who are upsetting me, who are not allowing us to return to normal life. There are so many other women here looking for jobs, but it's me whom you're, not interested in, but inquisitive about. Since I bear the title of Birangona given by the government. Your eyes, your behaviour, make it clear that I do not belong to your society. The government probably called us Birangona by mistake—what they meant was Barangana. Whores."

The man scribbled something on a piece of paper. Handing it to Yasmin, he said, "This is a letter for the clinic. You'd better go to them, *Ma*. You need treatment."

Yasmin's eyes flashed fire. "Pakistani soldiers damaged my body. And you people are damaging my mind. People like you, who are enjoying the fruits of independence without having had to give up anything. I'm told many people have been promoted in their jobs and now occupy important positions. No one is curious about them. But the whispers start no matter which office I set foot in. Everyone gathers around to gape at me."

Ripping up the piece of paper in the presence of the man who had scribbled the note, Yasmin went out on to the glaring sun-baked summer pavements. And then she wondered, where to now? Which way should she go? She remembered Tariq. They used to roam around as a pair at the university. Members of the same political party. Tariq would say, "I will always stand by you in bad times, Mina." Where was he today? He had gone off to fight in the war too. Not once had he come looking for Yasmin.

Chacha said, "What more can I do? You pick a fight wherever you go. People are saying you've gone mad."

Yasmin looked away in pain. "I wish I had. I wouldn't have had the ability to realise how shameless and cruel people can be."

Her uncle pretended to be sorry. "Whom can you single out? Your friend Tariq. He was talking about you too."

Yasmin was startled. "Is he alive?"

"He is. I believe he's got married. It's a trend nowadays for these young men to marry."

Yasmin was silent. She didn't say another word. Not even the most brutal piece of news in the world could affect her anymore.

Chacha said, "Tariq was saying it would be a good idea to arrange for you to get married too. The government is encouraging people to do this."

Yasmin was silent. She didn't say a word. She didn't speak for a long time.

She needed medical help to talk again. While she recovered, the enthusiasm about Birangonas died down. Finding new sources of excitement, people forgot the old one.

In the darkness, Marjina tells Huree, "Look how Yasmin Bu is thrashing about. Splash some water on her face."

Marjina strikes a match and lights a lamp. Pouring out a bowl of water, she splashes it on Yasmin's face. "What's wrong, *bu?*"

Yasmin collects herself slowly. Slurring her words, she says, "What was that sound, Huree?"

Huree says, "I don't know, I can't tell."

Everyone in the brothel is awake. Lights have come on in many of the rooms. Voices, conversations and anxious discussions among women of different ages rise over the sound of the rain. The azan at dawn is heard. A hint of light from an overcast sky breaks through the dark shadows in the lane. Everyone goes outside. What has happened becomes clear. A part of the roof of the decrepit old building has collapsed in the torrential rain. Three of the women are buried beneath the bricks and beams. Piru, Parul, Mamata.

Commotion spreads across the brothel. People throng the lane. Gazing with ashen faces at the debris of bricks and wood, the women discuss Piru, Parul and Mamata's fate in order to bury their anxieties about their own future. They have always known that any of their rooms can collapse from the rain. Still, the thought sends shivers down their spines at this moment.

The rain relents a little later in the day. Policemen arrive, followed by the fire-brigade. Labourers are put to the task of sifting through the debris to extricate the three women.

Jahanara says, "Do you suppose they're alive anymore? The room collapsed last night and they begin the rescue now in the afternoon."

Jahanara isn't the only one to think that way. Everyone says, "They must be dead."

Piru, Parul and Mamata's battered corpses are laid out in the middle of the lane. Everyone gathers around to stare in silence and fear. Mad Rohimon screams, "What are they staring at? What are all of them staring at? Everyone will meet the same fate someday. They were alive yesterday. They had customers in their room. Today, they're dead. We're not human. Humans don't die this way. Even dogs have a better death." The women, who have gathered in groups, look pale and pensive. Rohimon's delirious babble no longer seems incoherent. Their lives do seem uncertain. They're surviving on their bodies somehow, without food at times. They can be killed at any moment. By a knife, by an illness, by a room collapsing on them. They really aren't human beings. Mashi says sadly, "Mamata's business was flourishing. Fate wouldn't stand for it. This means losses for Hiru too."

Meanwhile, Phulmoti is trying to attract one of the labourers. "Come after you're done. I won't charge more than five taka."

The man strikes a deal for three, even as he's working. Piru, Parul and Mamata's corpses are still lying there. A police van takes them away before evening falls.

Bokul says, "They'll slice their bodies open now." Shanti asks in trepidation, "And then?"

Bokul cannot answer. No one knows for sure.

Darkness falls by the time the police, fire brigade and labourers leave. The listless women dress up mechanically, lighting incense sticks in their rooms, sprinkling a little extra holy water on themselves, and take their places in the lane. Although all of them are troubled to some extent by the incident, they have no choice. They need customers. Misery awaits them otherwise. Mannan lays out rows of paan with swift hands, sprinkling rosewater on them. The eunuchs had laid down their drums at Chheru's shop and were smoking anxiously. Chheru says, "What are all of you moping for? Let's start the singing. Nabu, Rocky, come on now." Getting to their feet, they begin to sway their bodies and sing like in the films. A couple of buyers turn up for hooch.

Huree comes up and tugs at one of them. The man is drunk already. Slurring his words, he says, "*Ei maagi!* You won't kill me beneath a collapsed roof, will you? I don't trust this fucking brothel."

Huree shoves the man into her room.

Marjina sneers, "You want a whore, but you're afraid for your life too. Only your lives are valuable, you bastards, not ours."

Still, business picks up, like during the closing hours on market day. Amidst the buying and selling and transfer of money, everyone forgets that three young women met untimely deaths in this brothel today. And yet the thorn of uncertainty continues to prick them, making them pensive every now and then.

SEVEN

Delwar visits quite often these days. He seems to have developed a kinship with all of them—Marjina, Huree, Shanti, Bokul, Kusum. In private, they refer to him as Yasmin Bu's man. But no one takes this seriously. Delwar mostly comes in the day time. He buys the women small gifts. Chats for hours with Yasmin over tea and cigarettes. They don't understand most of his conversations. But still, they like him. Because he's not like other men. Marjina says, "Do you think Dilu bhai will marry Yasmin, Huree?"

Huree mocks her, "What a stupid thing to say! Just because you like a whore, does it mean you have to marry her?"

Marjina doesn't accept defeat. "As if it doesn't. Didn't one of Rupa's lovers get her out of here? He married her too."

Marjina laughs. So does Huree, smoking. There's a reason for their laughter, though. Everyone had sighed when Rupa was taken away. All of them had envied her luck to some extent. Rupa came back a few months later. She took an entire room on rent from Kazi Shaheb and left again. Now she comes quite often. Dressed in a glittering sari and imitation jewellery, Rupa turns up in a burqa, her sandals squeaking, and unlocks the door with a key hanging from the end of her sari. She lights incense sticks inside.

Someone had once asked, "What's the matter, Rupa? Heart not in your beloved new home?"

Rupa had answered at once, "I'm not taking men at home. I'm doing it here. What to do, my husband doesn't earn enough. Many of the ladies in town have their private practices."

Home over there, customers here. Rupa maintains a balance between the two worlds.

Delwar is nearby. He overhears them. He asks, "Why do they hate marriage so much?"

Yasmin smiles, "They don't hate marriage, but they hate the idea of a whore's marriage. Like I do."

Delwar is silent. He knows everything about Yasmin's past now. He knows that someone had taken Yasmin away from the shelter for helpless women and married her. The news of this magnanimous marriage had been published prominently in the papers. But Yasmin had learnt the real objective of the marriage soon afterwards. She had found out that the "educated" gentleman already had a wife in his village. He had gained possession of Yasmin's father's house. And, how strange, Yasmin's uncle had gone to court demanding a share. Yasmin didn't know what deal the two of them had struck. The man had got Yasmin to sell the house. After which he had revealed his true colours. He had forced Yasmin to drink. And then enjoyed her all night in a group along with his friends.

She had tried to stop him. She had wept, fought. But a helpless Yasmin had only been beaten up cruelly in return. The man had mocked her, "If you could sleep with the Punjabi rogues, why not all this?"

Yasmin had fallen silent. He had brought in new people every day. All of them important people, she was told. The man had bartered her body for business contracts, becoming rich.

Then he had built another house and brought his wife, mother and sister from the village to live in it.

Yasmin has visited her uncle. He had turned away from her, saying that he was ashamed to disclose his blood relationship with a fallen woman.

She had visited her mother's brother. He and his wife had wrinkled their noses in revulsion. As though Yasmin were a worm from hell, even the sight of whom was sinful. All her uncle had said coldly was, "You sold your house and gave your Chacha his share of the money. Why are you here now? And besides, the past is past. You don't have a very good reputation in society now."

She had wanted to scream, "What is this society? The same society that had refused to lend a helping hand to a helpless woman, that would have murdered Yasmin if possible." Yasmin loathed the kind of society that purchased its freedom, its fame, in return for the life of a woman. She had returned to the prison that was her home with great anger, pain and resentment. There she had found her husband drinking with two well-dressed men. He had flown into a rage on seeing her. "Where did you go dressed so shabbily? Go and change your clothes. You have to go to Narayanganj with these gentlemen."

Standing at the door, Yasmin had declared with unshakeable determination. "I'll go. But not to Narayanganj."

Yasmin's husband had come up to her. "What are you saying? That's where the clients are."

Running his eyes over her body, one of the guests had said, "Charming woman. Let's not delay anymore."

Yasmin was resolute. "I'm going, but not with you."

Irked, Yasmin's husband had said, "Stop this nonsense. Have you any idea who these people are?"

Yasmin had not waited. Running down the stairs with fierce intent, she had wondered why the country and the society hadn't been pulverised into dust in the war.

Yasmin's husband had shouted at her to stop. She had not stopped. Seated in a rickshaw, she had muttered, "If the war has really turned me into a whore, why should I let the cream of society enjoy the fruits?

I'm a whore. I'll become a real one." Yasmin had moved into this brothel.

Delwar says softly, "I understand how much you resent the world, Yasmin."

Yasmin looks at him. "Not resentment. Call it hatred."

"Very well, hatred. But what's the use of destroying yourself ? You aren't like the rest of the women here, after all."

Yasmin smiles. "All your grand talk has got me worked up. I have to have some hooch today. Will you get me some?"

Delwar does not answer. Yasmin says, "Not just for myself, I want destruction for everyone. It is from destruction that a new life will emerge one day."

Pausing, she continues in a different tone, "Give me a cigarette." Delwar lights one for her. Exhaling smoke, Yasmin says, "I am not a human being, not a member of the society you come from. I am one of the women in this brothel. Those who cannot consider themselves human, who have forgotten how to do it."

Delwar's eyes hold pain. "Yasmin, you're explaining to them all the time that they're human beings too. Tell them they have to earn the right to be considered human."

Yasmin curls her lips. "Who will earn it? Those imprisoned in a jail made by animals?"

"It's not a joke, Yasmin. I know you can do it. I have seen a remarkable power in you. Don't you know that all prison walls crumble in the churnings of a revolution?"

Yasmin suddenly throws her cigarette away and sits up straight. "Can you tell me at what point a revolution begins?"

"I can. When injustice and tyranny are at their peak." Yasmin begins to laugh in a strange way.

Delwar stands up.

"I'll go now. It's time for your customers."

Jahanara stands at the head of the stairs, her eyes on Delwar. She calls Moyna. "O Moyna. This fellow has become a fixture here. Everyone likes him."

Moyna is busy, for she has to open her shop. With a quick smile she says, "Haven't you heard what he tells the girls?"

Jahanara frowns. "What does he say?"

Moyna rolls her eyes and sneers. "All my life I've heard whores do immoral things. Their lives on earth are black, their afterlives are dark. But listen to what he says. 'What makes you think all of you are committing a sin? It's people who have made you this way. You didn't do it by choice. If you have to answer, so do all of us.'"

Jahanara has no time for all this. She goes into her room. A beauteous darkness has descended on the blind lane. Jahanara lights incense sticks. She is expecting a juicy customer tonight. Kanchan has told her. But then all of Jahanara's customers are lucrative. Lawyers, journalists, poets, clerks, businessmen . . . all of them are her admirers. She also has other rich and powerful clients. Jahanara takes off the sari she is in and puts on a lacy red bra. About to put a new red chiffon sari on the bed, she jumps in alarm. Fat pustules have appeared on her arms. Her heart skips a beat. Everyone here knows the signs. Jahanara too. Has she then . . . No, it cannot be. But Jahanara feels vulnerable. Why can't it happen to her, considering where she is and what she does? With trembling hands, she takes off her clothes to examine her body. No, there can be no more doubt. The signs are there on her body too. Jahanara sits in her dark room, filled with foreboding. Many of the women in the brothel have had this illness. They conceal this dreaded, ugly disease as long as possible and keep plying their trade. Eventually it can no longer be kept under wraps. It reveals itself on the body. Someone plunders all the beauty and grace of the woman, like an merciless bandit. Poisonous sores fester on the body. The nose drops off. Her long years in this business have shown Jahanara many women who have rotted to death from this disease. Many have gone mad. Some have hanged themselves. Jahanara will meet the same fate. Her admirers will wrinkle their noses in disgust and desert her. There will be no more lucrative offers. Her earnings will dwindle. She will become an object of pity and charity. She cannot think anymore. Jahanara flings herself on her bed, clutches her pillow and begins to tremble. A fever seems about to invade her body.

Kanchan can be heard outside. "Jani! *Ei* Jani! Why is your room dark in the evening?"

Jahanara sits up in bed swiftly, covers her arms and legs with her sari and says, "Come in, Kanchan."

Kanchan enters. "What's the matter, Janu?"

Jahanara is silent for a while. Then she says despondently, "I won't take in customers today. Not feeling well."

Kanchan is furious. "You think you can do as you please? I've got hold of a fat customer. You can't just say no."

Jahanara does not get angry. She says, exhausted, "I can't today. Say no to him."

Kanchan jerks Jahanara upright. He says, "Let me tell you, Jani, these moods will be the end of you. It's a lot of money, I've taken an advance too. Now you're saying no. Get up. Turn on the light. I'm going now. I have to bring him from the hotel."

Kanchan leaves. Wearily, Jahanara gets out of bed. Switching on the light, she puts on her expensive petticoat and sari and proceeds to rub powder on her face. After all these years, she feels disgusted with herself, with her room, with her profession. Completing her make-up, she fetches the bottle of liquor sitting on the shelf. There's only a little bit left. Pouring it down her throat, Jahanara feels her eyes growing moist. She mutters to herself, "You'll die too, just like Rohimon. You'll rot to death. Not even the dogs in the lane will turn to look at you."

Overcome with self-pity, Jahanara bursts into tears all alone in her room.

EIGHT

Kusum feels very tired as she stands in the lane. She hasn't been well for the past few months. She gets a low fever every morning and evening. She has a persistent cough too. An ache weighs down her back and chest. She's in a daze for a long time every morning when she wakes up. For the past few days she has been coughing up blood. Kusum hasn't told anyone. Still, despite her tiredness, she has to take her place in the lane with everyone else. She must take in customers. Kusum has withered. She needs many tricks and much effort to snare a customer these days. She hasn't had one for two days now. She more or less starved both those days. Kusum no longer enjoys being tormented by Kalu. She can't take it anymore. Today she's been lucky enough to get a customer very quickly. They settle for three taka. Kusum wanted five. She leads the way. The rent for Zarina's room has gone up. So Kalu has moved Kusum to Yasmin's room. The door is closed. Maybe Yasmin has a customer.

Huree and Marjina are bargaining in the lane. Kusum knocks on the door. "O *bu*, come out quick. I have a customer waiting."

Kusum's customer is getting impatient. He presses her sickly thin body, draped in a dirty, tattered sari, to his breast right there outside the door, running his hand all over her lecherously. Suddenly he says, "Why is your body so hot?"

Kusum is startled. She is afraid. What if the man disappears on knowing she is not well? She summons a carefree tone to her voice. Touching his lips with her hot ones like an accomplished seductress, she says, "My body is always hot."

After a pause, she says with an arch look, "Do you want a woman as cold as a fish?"

Yasmin isn't opening the door. Some sort of heated argument is going on inside. Yasmin is shouting at the top of her voice. A male voice can be heard now and then. Kusum is astonished. Yasmin Bu never quarrels with anyone. Least of all with customers. Eavesdropping, Kusum hears her enraged voice, "Why did you fight the other day, for whom?"

Marjina appears with a customer. She says, "What's this, Kusum, why are you still waiting here? If one person is going to monopolise the room, how will we entertain our customers?"

She bangs on the door. "Open the door, *bu*. We're getting late." Still, the door doesn't open. There are sounds of a scuffle inside.

Marjina and Kusum both feel scared. Huree comes running too from somewhere. All three of them begin to bang on the door. A hinge breaks and the broken door opens with a crack, hanging on one side. All three of them blanch at the sight. A well-dressed young man is sitting holding his head. Blood is flowing all over his face from a cut on his forehead. The three of them are bewildered for a moment. Kusum and Marjina's customers have slunk away at all this. Yasmin is standing with her back to the wall, panting, the end of her sari on the floor. Leave alone Marjina, Huree or Kusum, no one in the brothel has seen Yasmin like this. A broken bottle is rolling in the dust. Marjina enters and takes a close look at the man by the light of the lamp. He seems to belong to a decent family. He's dressed in expensive clothes, with long flowing hair, sideburns and a moustache. A handsome young man. Why should someone like him be bleeding from the forehead? How has he cut it? Is it Yasmin, then? And why is he sitting there so guiltily? His fancy shirt is soaked in blood. Marjina asks Yasmin softly, "What's the matter, bu?" Yasmin turns towards her and says vehemently, "Take a look, see for yourself. I broke a bottle on his head. I would have killed him if I could have."

Yasmin bites her lip to control her anger and agitation. She says, "So you've come to a brothel for some fun with whores? How much money have you amassed from your crimes, Kamal?"

The man lifts his eyes momentarily before lowering them again. He does not speak. Marjina, Huree and Kusum are perplexed. Yasmin seems to be boiling with rage. She continues scathingly, "I read about bank robberies and law-breaking in the papers all the time. I believe there are some misguided youth among the criminals. You too . . . "

Kamal looks at her. "You can do what you like to me, Yasmin. But I really did not know I am responsible for your situation today."

Yasmin flies into a temper. "You don't have to worry about what's happened to me. The you I see today is not the person we gave shelter to. We gave sanctuary to a freedom fighter who went to war for the country, for the people. For whom I lost my parents, my brothers and sisters. And became a whore."

Resentment and unhappiness are melded in Kamal's voice. "Yasmin, those who have made you a whore are the same people who have destroyed me. Today I gamble for thousands of taka. I'm dying of alcohol abuse. I am seeking life in the taste of women's flesh. I . . . I needn't have been this way. Who were the people who pushed me in this direction when I came back from the war?"

Yasmin looks unwaveringly at Kamal. "Don't try to fool your conscience with all this, Kamal. There are many other freedom fighters in the country who have not gone your way. They are still leading healthy lives."

The blood is trickling from Kamal's forehead down his cheek. There's an impossible agony in his voice, "I don't deny what you're saying. But I also know that if my role was at the root of the plight you are in today, it has become insignificant in comparison to the injustice of society. It is a section of the same society that could not accept you easily which used disillusioned young men like us as weapons to push us towards destruction. We are killing ourselves."

A peculiar smile appears on Yasmin's face. "Men are not in chains the way women are. A man who cannot use his power to protest against injustice and wrongdoing deserves to die."

Kamal lifts his eyes in surprise. And then lowers them at once. Quite a crowd has gathered outside the room by now. Everyone has come to know that Yasmin has smashed a bottle on a customer's head. Mashi appears at the door, hands on her hips. "What is it, woman? What's all this? We'll get a bad name if you behave this way."

Kamal rises to his feet in discomfort.

Yasmin goes up to him. "Wait. Wipe your forehead before you leave."

Tearing off a part of her sari, Yasmin wipes the blood off Kamal's face. Then she says, "Go now. If anyone asks, tell them you had an accident. A major accident."

Kamal leaves guiltily, his eyes downcast. Mashi enters the room at once. "What is it? Were you drunk?"

Yasmin tells herself rather than Mashi, "No. There was an incident a long time ago. And today there was an accident."

Mashi leaves in annoyance. "The woman is so drunk she's speaking in English."

Yasmin emerges from her room, torn apart by a great pain. The money Kamal gave her is bundled into her sari. What is Yasmin to do with this accursed money? Should she rip up the notes and throw them into the drain? But why? The money might have come from the illegal income of a freedom fighter sinking into the debris, but for Yasmin, it's her earnings. Yasmin walks up to Phulmoti's room. Phulmoti doesn't have a customer. She probably hasn't been able to get one. Putting her baby on a torn quilt on top of a mat, she is trying to get her to sleep. Sitting with her legs sprawled out, she is probing her hair for lice with one hand while stroking the baby lightly with the other, humming a lullabye out of tune. In the light of the soot-covered lamp in the dirty room, the starving, penniless whore Phulmoti's face looks extraordinarily tender.

As though she is not Phulmoti the starving, penniless whore, but Phulmoti the mother. Nothing but a mother. She does not know who the father of the baby is. Humming gently, the soft-eyed Phulmoti has become a picture of the Madonna. A wonderful, soothing breeze blows over the agony in Yasmin's heart. She gazes at Phulmoti and her child.

Millions of mothers in this neighbourhood, this city, this country, this world, are singing lullabyes to their children, dreaming of their growing up as happy and successful human beings. Perhaps some of them will be lost. But some will hold their heads up high. They will be human beings. Nothing but human beings.

Phulmoti turns towards Yasmin. "Who's there?"

Yasmin returns to the present with a start. Tossing the money into Phulmoti's lap, she says, "Keep this. Buy milk for the baby."

Kusum cannot get out of bed the next morning. Her body is wracked by a high fever. She is coughing continuously and is delirious. "Ma. Ma. Where are you?"

Huree is on her way to wash her clothes. She says ruefully, "As if we have mothers."

Marjina says, "The girl is lying on the floor. She has a cough. The cold will make it worse. Should we take her to Shanti's room? Shanti is on holiday. Her room is empty."

Not a bad idea, thinks Yasmin. Shanti's on holiday, which means she has gone home to her village for a fortnight. Yasmin says, "Ask Mashi. She has the key. I'll send Delwar for the doctor when he comes."

At this, Marjina cups her face in her palm. "What are you saying? Since when has anyone in this brothel ever gone to a doctor when ill? If their fate decrees it, they survive; if not, they die. The *dom* takes the corpse away."

Kusum begins to cough uncontrollably in her fever. Her tiny, scrawny body bends like a bow with the ferocity of the cough. A worried Yasmin rubs her chest and back. Kusum is tossing and turning. Suddenly her body is convulsed by a severe bout of coughing. Blood is spurting from her mouth as she coughs. The oily quilt and pillow are soaked.

Marjina moans, "Oh god, what's this! Blood from her mouth."

Yasmin wipes Kusum's face swiftly with a corner of the sheet. "Marjina, check if there's any mustard oil in the bottle. Warm it, I'll massage her chest and back with it."

Marjina says sadly, "How will I have any oil? So expensive! Let me see if Bokul has some."

Kusum is curled up, inanimate. There are bloodstains on her cheeks. Marjina returns a little later with a few drops of oil in a dented enamel bowl. Lighting the stove to warm it, she says, "Bokul isn't human. I asked for a few drops of oil, how she sneered at me. 'You think I spend money on oil to throw it away!' You tell me, *bu*, she's hot property right now, she can afford fish and meat every day, but why all this arrogance? No one can say whose fortune will plummet tomorrow."

Yasmin begins to massage Kusum's chest and back with warm oil. Leaning over her, she calls, "Kusum! *Ei* Kusum!"

Kusum is lying inert. She opens her eyes with great effort. She cannot talk.

Marjina sighs as she leaves. "Accursed house. Those who live here are worse than cats and dogs. No one will know even if they scream all the way to their deaths."

Delwar arrives in the afternoon. He fetches a doctor. Examining Kusum carefully, the doctor says, "She has to be taken to a hospital. Needs a blood-test. An X-Ray. And she'll only get worse in this damp room with no fresh air."

Delwar pays the doctor's fees and gets the preliminary medicines he's prescribed.

Kalu finds out and arrives to make a huge fuss. He flings Kusum's quilt away and kicks her all but unconscious body. Glaring at Delwar, he says, "Who are you to fuck around here? Whose woman are you taking to the hospital? I bought her with my own money, who dares take her out of here?"

Delwar has built a rapport with the local hoodlums in the course of his regular visits here. He reaches out for Kalu's arm. "She will die if she isn't taken to the hospital. And besides, she has the coughing illness. Others will get it too."

In a foul mood, Kalu shouts, "To hell with your doctors. Two kicks and she'll be fine."

Yasmin steps forward. "Kalu! No one cares for the women here even if they're dying. Someone is trying to arrange for her treatment. Why are you stopping him?"

A buzz rises amongst the women who have gathered. They're speaking softly, but they all support the idea of Kusum's being taken to a hospital.

Kalu is furious. He says, "I get it. It was a big mistake to let Kusmi stay in this *bibi*'s room. Now she's here in a group to lecture me."

In full view of everyone's incredulous eyes, Kalu drags Kusum, who is now all but unconscious, by the feet to Zarina's room. He says, "I'm leaving her with you, Zari. If anyone comes near her, tell them I'll put a knife in their belly."

Kalu goes out and lights a cigarette he has got from Mannan's shop. The gathering disperses, but the discussions go on for a long time. Some blame Kalu. Others pass snide comments about Yasmin and Delwar's excessive concern.

Smoking, Mashi says, "She belongs to Kalu, he can do what he wants. What can anyone else have to say about it?"

Zarina is the first to flare up in anger. Going to Yasmin's room, she says, "Just tell me and I'll have that bastard murdered, Yasmin Bu. The girl is coughing up blood."

Pushing the stove away, Marjina wheels around. "Why? Are we like dead dogs whose bodies anyone within reach can maul as they please?" Huree snarls too, "We sell our bodies. Don't we have some rights over those bodies?"

Yasmin is stupefied. Delwar is sitting on the cot, an embodiment of helplessness.

Yasmin looks at Huree. "Each of you is responsible for your condition today."

Bokul appears at the door. She says, "How many of us are here out of free will? It's people like Kalu who got hold of us and brought us here." Delwar opens a magazine he has brought and holds it out to Yasmin.

"Look, this magazine has written in detail about the plight of the women here. It's created a stir among people. Only sensible people, of course."

Yasmin takes the magazine and reads aloud, "Dhaka's Home of Sex Workers."

Bokul, Marjina, Huree gather around Yasmin. "What have they written, *buji*?"

Yasmin scans the piece. "About us. About our misery."

Marjina says in surprise, "Really?"

"Yes. Maybe people are thinking about us nowadays."

Their eyes grow moist. They are all moved by Kusum's condition. Yasmin sees a desperate hope in their sorrowful faces and teary eyes. When she had been telling them about how women in other countries had escaped their misery, she had seen disbelief and confusion in their foolish glances. Perhaps consorting with Delwar and the proximity with Yasmin have given them a faint beam of hope that says they can consider themselves human beings. But they do not know where to find the unbarred door that will let them stand up for their rights as humans. They do not know how to pass through that door.

Yasmin says, "Take Kusum's medicines with you, Zari. I'll tell you when she has to have them."

Zarina leaves with an air of solidarity.

Reading the magazine, Yasmin says, "You think your responsibility is discharged by talking of Dhaka's brothels only. Who will speak up for the millions of women around the world who are suffering in hell the same way?"

The other women leave after a while. Leafing through the magazine, Yasmin stops at a particular spot. The usual sneering smile flashes at the corners of her lips. "I see the women in your society are deeply involved in feminism. I read about it all the time. What do you think freedom for women means?"

Delwar smiles too. "Feminism is a wave all over the world now. Our women are adding their voices to the chorus of slogans to become modern."

Yasmin crumples the magazine and throws it in a corner. "Do those who are participating in this revolution know how many women are living like prisoners, victims of perverted male desire? In the olden days, not even the maids in the harems lived in such misery."

Delwar smiles again. "They don't keep track of all this. Rich housewives are seeking freedom for women through meetings and conferences and seminars. They are busy with equal rights for women when it comes to jobs, education, offices, even the home."

Yasmin scolds him. "Don't laugh. Tell them about Kusum, tell them about Piru and Mamata and Parul, tell them about the women in thousands of brothels like this one. If you can, ask them whether they have the courage to snatch genuine freedom for women from the clutches of men."

Delwar stands up. "I have to go now. I'm leaving some books behind, read them if you can. I'll be back tomorrow. Let me try to persuade Kalu about Kusum."

Kusum dies early the next morning, before Delwar arrives. With mute, lifeless eyes, all the women stare at her famished, humiliated figure. A lament rises in everyone's heart. But it does not penetrate the casing of their bodies to break down the barriers of the decrepit buildings on either side of the lane and reach the world outside. Like many other incidents, people forget about Kusum too in a few days.

Only when a young girl asks Mannan for credit in the afternoon, or when the eunuchs make vulgar contortions and sing film songs at Chheru's buzzing liquor dive, or when the women line up in the lane and the customers arrive and someone in a grimy sari, unkempt hair, malnourished body and unblossomed womanhood chases a man, plucking at his sleeve and reciting a monotonous litany of her physical prowess—that is when Yasmin is startled. She remembers Kusum then. Gazing at the narrow slice of a starry sky, Yasmin wonders pensively, how much longer must these incarcerated women waste away as they bear the burden of their intolerable lives?

NINE

The sunlight dies above two rows of hideous, dilapidated terraces. Daylight lies discarded like the curled up skin of a dead snake within the damp, dark, dirty brothel. Jahanara begins to fade too. Her lustre diminishes. Sores appear all over her body like venomous abscesses. They call it a summer rash. Many of the women here suffer from this disease. And yet Jahanara's illness is a matter of great curiosity to many.

Those who have been envying the rise in her fortunes are simply contemptuous now. "Where have all the wealthy customers gone? What's happened to all those saris and the jewellery she used to flaunt, all those jaunts in cars? Those days are gone. As they do for everyone. A whore's fate is like the full moon and the new moon."

Jahanara puts on a burqa and visits a doctor once a week. The doctor has said it will be cured. Jahanara gazes wistfully. What if it is cured? Her business is ruined. All her regular customers visit Bokul now. The honeybees who used to buzz around her when she was in full bloom have flown away. A sick Jahanara lies all alone on her bed. Moyna no longer cleans her room. The dilapidated room looks as pathetic as an ugly woman past her prime. Jahanara weeps. She sends for hooch and for *bilati*. Moyna has to be cajoled to fetch her the bottle. If she reminds Moyna too many times, she snarls from downstairs, "How can I run to the shop fifty times for you? My time is valuable."

Jahanara loses her temper now and then. She abuses Moyna and everyone else in the filthiest of language. She is furious with the whole world. One day she pounces on the nude on the wall and rips it to pieces. Then, cursing the former lovers of her body by name, the helpless, friendless Jahanara beats her head against the wall.

Mashi rebuilds the room that Piru, Parul and Mamata used to live in. Hiru has brought a striking young girl. The sixteen-year-old is voluptuous enough to pass off for a full-blown twenty-two-year-old woman. Hiru has bought her for eight hundred taka from the pimp at Taanbazar. He has told Mashi, "What a dish I've got. Golapi will become another Jahanara before the year passes."

Her name is Golapi. No one gets to know where she's from, or how she fell into the clutches of a pimp.

A confused and bewildered Golapi seems to lose her power of speech as soon as she enters the brothel. She does not budge at all. Only helpless tears stream from her eyes.

Marjina says, "What's the use of crying, my love? It'll do you no good even if you flood the place with your tears and break your heart." Golapi does not say a word to anyone. Hiru has her lunch sent from the restaurant. She does not even touch it. Rohimon swoops down on her plate and makes off with it. Devouring it by the drain, she says,

"The dogs would have eaten it if I didn't."

Old Golapjaan casts covetous glances at the food from a distance. Rohimon abuses her, "Die, you bitch. Can't death get you? Kusum died. All the young girls like Mamata and Piru died. But you don't die, you hag. You languish here by the drain but your heart keeps beating. What use is it for you to be alive?"

Golapjaan spits and says something incoherently. Quickly putting some food in her mouth and shielding the plate, Rohimon says, "Don't you dare abuse me, *maagi*. I'm dying of hunger and this is mine."

Walking past, Huree says, "She's dead already. Why abuse her anymore?"

Hiru brings some friends before darkness falls. They're as fierce as he is. One of them has an expensive bottle of imported liquor beneath his arm. Hiru drags Golapi over to a room.

Mashi says, "No treat for us when you break her in, Hiru?"

Hiru glares at her. "See how adamant the bitch looks? Let me fix her first."

Mashi chuckles, smoking. "Even when you buy a chicken, you have to keep it tied up for the first two days. Then it goes into the coop on its own. She'll be fine in a couple of days."

Hiru and his friends enter the room with Golapi.

The women are busy preparing for the evening. Yasmin is lying in bed, reading a book in the fading light. Combing her hair, Marjina says gloomily, "It'll be Judgment Day for that girl today. She's new, and on top of that three or four huge men are in the room with her."

Yasmin is absorbed in her book. She does not pay attention to Marjina. Huree enters a little later. She says, "The girl is screaming so much. Poor thing. She's saying, 'I've never had a drink. Don't force me.' Three or four of them have grabbed her and are pouring it down her throat. What choice does she have?"

Suddenly Golapi's stricken cries spread across the dank, half-dark lane. Everyone trembles, recalling their own similar, bitter memories. They all know how she will be tortured now.

Her screams smash against the wall again. Yasmin's senses recoil from her book into the hard reality of the darkness.

Yasmin stands up with the book in her hand. Anger coursing through her body like an uncontrollable stream of lava, she asks Huree, "How many of them?"

Marjina answers, "I saw three or four."

Yasmin is shaking with blind rage. She says, "What can they do if all the women in the brothel attack them?"

Marjina looks at her in consternation. "Have you gone mad, Yasmin Bu? Hiru has bought her, he can do as he pleases with her, what's it got to do with us?"

This doesn't quell Yasmin. "No one in the world owns anyone else, Marjina."

Huree is annoyed. She says, "We don't understand all this. This is stuff from your books. How can we fight against those rogues?"

Yasmin flies into a temper. "Are you two coming with me or not?" Marjina grips her arm. "Sit down. Don't lose your head. How can

you be so reckless when you've been here so long? Don't you know how many people they have killed?"

Golapi's helpless screams revolve around the brothel, bouncing from one room to the next. They seem to drive Yasmin mad. Impossible. Intolerable. No more of this. Protest is essential. How much longer must women scream in futility after becoming the victims of bestial behaviour from perverted men? Yasmin rushes out of the room and races up the stairs. Practically all the women in the area have gathered outside. Everyone is anticipating with terror the inevitability of something horrible. Yasmin pushes the door open violently. At once, she is rendered speechless by an inhuman scene. A devastated, naked woman is running around the room, weeping piteously, "Let me go. You're like my father, you're like my brother. For Allah's sake."

Intoxicated by lust, the four men have turned into savage beasts. Two of them push her down to the floor. One of them places his foot on her uncovered breasts. Hiru is drinking in a corner and laughing. Yasmin screams, covering her face with her hands. Two other elderly women have followed Yasmin upstairs. Mashi tugs at her from the back. "Come away. Come away. Don't create trouble here."

Yasmin shouts at the top of her voice, "No."

Everyone in the room turns towards her. One of the men says in a drunken stupor, "Another one of the bitches here. Get her inside. More fun."

Another man drags Yasmin into the room. The book in her hand is flung to the floor.

As soon as this happens, the other women on the veranda and the staircase explode.

Marjina, Huree, Shanti, Bokul all begin to shout.

Zarina says, "If you hurt Yasmin Bu, we will kill you, Hiru."

Hiru shuts the door in the face of their screams and shouts. A commotion ensues. Hiru is furious at their revelry being interrupted. Coming out of the room, he barks at them, "Get out of here, you bitches. Or else you'll see what happens."

Someone speaks up from the gathering of women. "What will you do? There are just the four of you. So many of us women. Even if each of us slaps you once, you'll become mash."

Mashi begins to abuse the women. "You line of whores, what do you think you're doing! You've become too big for your own good. I'm informing the police at once. They eat out of my hands. They'll beat all of you to a pulp."

Marjina stands up to her. "To hell with your police. You scare us with talk of the police to extort money from us every month. You think we don't understand?"

The women are flinging themselves at the door. Like a dormant volcano suddenly become active.

Mashi shouts in agitation, "Your tongues are loose today, you bitches. I'm calling the goons right now. Go back, all of you. Go back." Zarina looks at her with blazing eyes. "Do what you can, we aren't

afraid anymore."

Huree pushes through the crowd. Planting a kick on the door, she says, "You *khankir poot* Hiru, you son of a whore, let Yasmin Bu out. Or you'll see what happens."

Opening the door, Hiru charges at them ferociously. "What will you do, you swine women? I'll slit all your throats and dump the lot of you in the drain."

Zarina shouts back, hands on her hips, "We'll set the room on fire. We'll burn the brothel down."

Moyna quips, "Good idea. Your own rooms will burn down. Business will go to hell. You'll burn to death."

Moyna and Marjina begin to argue. Some of the women rush towards Moyna threateningly. And at that moment, a scream of pain is heard. At once, the women break the door down. The men race out. The flames of revolt are stilled. The women are silent. Hiru is standing in the middle of the room. Yasmin is bathed in blood at his feet.

Under everyone's terrified eyes, Yasmin's half-naked body, with a knife plunged into the stomach, writhes once or twice before turning lifeless. Hiru's eyes are bloodshot.

Hiru pulls the knife out, tears a page out of Yasmin's book lying on the floor, wipes the blood off the blade with it, crumples it into a ball and flings it at the stunned women.

As he leaves the room, he says, "Look, you whores. See for yourself what Hiru can do."

The women retreat. They gaze at Yasmin's corpse with the agonised eyes of defeated, beaten up animals. The blood-soaked page from the book lies in front of them. They can only see the blood on one side of the page. They do not know that on the other side is printed the well- known saying: "Man is born free, and everywhere he is in chains."

Somewhere in the silenced, stupefied building, a baby's cry of independent protest rings out. Phulmoti's baby is crying at the top of her voice.